THE ASSIGNMENT

Tracey Sutton

I can do all things through
Christ which strengtheneth me.
Philippians 4:13

ACKNOWLEDGMENTS

First and foremost, I give all the glory and praise to God, for giving me the perseverance and determination to complete this novel. Writing this book was a challenge, and there were countless times when I doubted my ability to see this dream come to fruition. I feel immensely blessed to have received an abundance of support from family and friends.

To my husband, Eric: Thank you for your infinite patience and believing in me. You were always there, cheering me on, and offering praise and encouragement. I couldn't have done this without your support.

A special thanks to my grandparents, Earl and Bobbie, for instilling the importance of faith in me. The world is a better place because of you.

My deep appreciation to my editor, Dr. Bonnie Harvey, for polishing my manuscript and providing the guidance I needed. I have learned so much from you, and I look forward to working on the next project together.

A special thanks to my Mom and in-laws for encouraging me to follow my dreams. It has been a long three years, but now I can say, "Look Mom; I did it. Dreams really do come true."

Sincerely, and more than I can express, my gratitude to Vince and Mark for critiquing my work and providing friendships that I will cherish forever.

Finally, a very special thank you to Misty and Roberta, two of my biggest fans. You will never know how much your support has meant to me. You were the angels sitting on my shoulder.

CHAPTER ONE

"Not tonight," Annie sighed as she scribbled the words onto the paper. She didn't want to be rude, but she couldn't allow herself to be happy. Today…she would mourn. Her mind drifted back to that horrible day, four years ago, when someone told her that her mother had been killed. A drunk driver crossed the centerline. Annie bit the corner of her lip as the police officer's voice haunted her memory again. Going on a date was the last thing on her mind. She just wanted to be left alone.

The force from the pen created a mess of ink as it leaked onto the white paper and the edge of her palm. Annie looked around the classroom to see if anyone was looking before she wet her finger and began wiping the black streaks from her hand.

The open classroom windows brought in the smell of honeysuckle, making it obvious that spring had arrived. Annie smiled as she watched the squirrels playing on the front lawn of the university. Then her smile slowly faded as feelings of guilt entered her mind.

She folded the letter and passed it back to Mark. He had a crush on her since the ninth grade. Annie winced at his frown and knew that her rejection hurt him…again. She despised hurting his feelings, but she had no interest in getting serious with anyone. She knew that the anniversary of her mother's death caused her emotions to run wild. Taking a chance on being vulnerable wasn't something she was willing to do.

The sound of the bell startled her. "How boring was that?" Kim asked. Kim had been Annie's best friend since fifth grade. People always thought of them as the odd couple because they were so different. Kim was tall, blonde, and very outgoing. Annie, on the other hand, was only five-foot-two, brunette, and extremely introverted. People referred to her as "little Annie" because of her petite frame. Kim tried repeatedly to convince Annie to try out for cheerleading, during their Freshman year of high school, but Annie refused. Instead, she joined the band and played the clarinet so they could go to the away games together. Kim cheered as she watched Annie march during the half-time shows. Annie recited all of the cheers from the stands as she watched Kim and the other girls form pyramids.

"To be honest with you, I didn't pay much attention," Annie remarked.

"Having second thoughts about going out with Mark?" Kim asked.

"Don't start, I'm..."

Before Annie could respond, Kim rolled her eyes. "I know, I know. You're not looking for a serious relationship," she said in a sarcastic tone. "You know you're going to have to give someone a chance someday, Annie."

Annie hated when Kim pressured her about finding a boyfriend. She breathed a sigh of relief as they entered the parking lot because she could escape the conversation. She was even more thankful they didn't park near each other. "I'll call you later," Annie said.

The warm air felt refreshing as the sun glistened on her face. Annie opened the passenger door and placed her books on the seat. As she struggled to remove the tight sleeve from her arm, Kim drove by. "Remember what I said." Annie tossed the sweater into the car, pretending not to acknowledge her friend's comment.

Annie drove home with the windows down. She wanted to enjoy the ambiance of spring in the North Georgia mountains. Dahlonega came to life this time of year. The small college town resembled a ghost town during the winter months. Tourists made their last journeys to Dahlonega during the fall to drive through the mountains and take in the beauty of the leaves as they transformed into shades of copper, gold, and crimson. The entire community embraced spring with open arms, as if it were a long-lost friend. The small shops on the town square had their doors propped open and the cafés and ice cream parlor posted daily specials in the windows. The Dogwood and Cherry trees bloomed in all their glory and the azaleas planted around the courthouse gained recognition from tourists, as well as local newspapers.

Annie's eyes filled with tears as she drove through the cemetery. She knew her father had placed a bouquet of yellow flowers on the grave. Her mother loved the color yellow. Annie and her father joked about it, but her mother always said, "Yellow signifies happiness." Annie wiped the corner of her eyes to stop the tears from flowing. Her throat felt tight, but she managed to force a hoarse whisper from within.

"I miss you so much, Mom." She knelt down to straighten the flowers. "Dad misses you too. I know…he talks to you every night. I hear him." The tears began to flow uncontrollably, as her cries grew louder. Annie rested her head against the tombstone. She longed to have her mother's arms around her again, if only for a minute. "I better go," she whispered, "Dad needs me." She brushed the loose-cut grass from her pants and made her way back to the car.

****

Annie was studying at the dining room table when she heard the front door open.

"Annie," her father called.

"In here, Daddy."

"Hope you're hungry," he said, as he walked into the room with a bag of food from Bill's Barbecue.

Annie knew he was trying to be strong, but his red, swollen eyes depicted the truth. Jack had changed since his wife's death. Basically, he just existed in a world of loneliness. Although they always needed extra money, everyone knew he took a second job to stay busy. He and his wife epitomized the perfect marriage. They were high school sweethearts and this was evident in all of their pictures in the yearbook. Annie's mother had written, "Jack and Ann forever" on several pages. Since the accident, Annie couldn't bear to look at the yearbook. Her heart ached at the unfair reality of their separation. She dreamed about finding a love that strong, but never imagined it could be possible.

"Yum," Annie said, as she closed her notebook and followed him into the kitchen. After dinner, she headed upstairs to relax with a nice, hot bubble bath. As she rested her head on the soft, bath pillow, she raised her foot to examine the pedicure she had gotten the day before. Annie smiled as she thought about ignoring her friend in the parking lot. Kim was determined to hook Annie up with Mark. He was nice, but not what Annie had pictured as Mr. Right. He had a sense of humor, but his idea of excitement was refurbishing computers. He wore round-rimmed glasses and kept his blond hair parted neatly on the side. Kim was convinced he was the guy for Annie.

The water began to lose its warmth and Annie wanted to call Kim before she curled into bed with her new book. Annie dreaded going to class the next day because Kim wouldn't be there. She had an appointment to get her wisdom teeth removed. Annie promised to take notes in Sociology, their favorite class, and of course fill Kim in on any gossip that took place.

CHAPTER TWO

As the rain spilled down the large windows of the classroom, Annie watched as some of her classmates entered the room with soaked clothes. She was thankful her two previous classes had been in the Owens Hall building or she would have been drenched as well. As she stared out the window, she hoped the rain would let up by the time class finished.

Annie reached into her book bag to retrieve her notebook and pen when Mr. Riley entered the room, carrying his usual cup of tea. "Good afternoon, class."

As he took a sip of tea, he flipped through the pages of the textbook. "Let's begin where we left off with examining behavioral patterns of various age groups and how society portrays these groups." He looked around the room before continuing. "What if I were to ask you if it would be viewed the same if a toddle threw a temper tantrum versus a ten year old?"

Just as he began to expound on the subject, the door opened. All eyes turned to focus on the figure standing in the doorway. In walked a student, but not a familiar face. He was tall with a medium build and his dark, wavy hair barely touched his collar. Although, Annie sat in the back of the room, she could see his crystal, blue eyes from a distance. He wore a white button-down shirt, khaki pants and loafers.

He ran his fingers through his damp hair, as he handed Mr. Riley a slip of paper.

"Okay, class, this is Dan Wilson. He will be joining our class this semester."

Mr. Riley looked around the room for an empty seat. "Take a seat in the back row," he said, as he pointed to the empty chair next to Annie.

Her heart began to beat faster as this new guy...Dan Wilson walked toward her. He removed his backpack and slid into the chair next to her. He didn't say a word or attempt to make eye contact. His cologne smelled good, but Annie felt nervous with him sitting next to her. She wondered if she should move into Kim's empty seat. *No, I can't do that,* Annie thought. That would be rude. From the corner of her eye, she could see him running his fingers through his hair. She pretended to concentrate on the lecture, but it was very difficult. Dan was so amazingly good-looking.

The clock on the wall read five till four and it was hard to believe an hour had passed.

"Read chapters two and three and answer the discussion questions by Thursday," Mr. Riley said. "I will be assigning your project for the semester so make sure you read the chapters."

At the sound of the bell, Dan leaned over to place his book in the backpack. He stood up, situated the bag on his back, and walked toward the door. He hadn't given Annie even a glance during the entire class.

"Bye to you too," Annie whispered under her breath. She couldn't wait to tell Kim about the new guy...Dan Wilson.

****

Kim was lying on her bed watching television when Annie peeked around the door that was only half closed.

"Knock, knock," Annie said. "Could you stand some company?"

Kim lifted her hand and mumbled something that resembled "hey." Her mouth was still stuffed with gauze from the surgery.

"Your mom said it went well," Annie said.

Kim nodded. Her eyes drooped and her cheeks were swollen. Annie sat on the bed next to her and flipped through her notebook to find the notes she copied.

"You're not going to believe it but we have a new guy in Sociology," Annie said. "Oh, and take a guess where he sat?"

Kim shifted her eyes from the television to Annie.

"Not only that, he is extremely and I mean extremely cute," Annie said.

Kim's eyes widened in disbelief as if begging for more details. "Tell me, tell me," she mumbled.

Annie described every detail in great length from what he was wearing to the scent of his cologne. "Oh," Annie paused, "his name is Dan Wilson. He didn't seem very friendly, though."

"Maybe he was just nervous," Kim muttered.

"I don't know, but I'm not going to go out of my way to talk to him," Annie said.

Kim rolled her eyes. "See, that's what I'm talking about," she said.

Annie ignored Kim's comment. "Well, I better get home and start on my homework. Oh, that reminds me. We have to read chapters two and three and answer the discussion questions by Thursday. Riley said he would be assigning our project for the semester."

****

Later that evening, Annie struggled to read chapter two. It was too difficult to concentrate. Despite reading the same words over and over, she couldn't comprehend anything. Her mind was preoccupied as she thought about Sociology class. "Dan Wilson," she whispered.

She traced his name in her notebook and wrote her name under the "a" in Dan, as if it were a line on a crossword puzzle. She pressed her lip against the paper, marveling at the lip print that surrounded their names. She decided to get ready for bed since she couldn't concentrate. After brushing her teeth and going through the nightly ritual of brushing her hair and removing her make-up, she opened the closet door. She wondered if she would run into Dan the next day or if she would have to wait until Thursday to see him. She needed to find something decent to wear just in case.

CHAPTER THREE

English Composition and Calculus were the only classes Annie had on Wednesdays. She decided that since she had four hours before her next class, she would go to the library and study. She and Kim usually went into town to eat lunch at the Big Bear Café after English class, but Kim didn't feel well and went home. Annie could sympathize with her because she remembered how she felt when her wisdom teeth were pulled. She didn't feel like eating for a week.

The library was crowded and it was evident that people used it as a social gathering. Unable to concentrate, Annie gathered her books and went outside. It was a beautiful day and certainly warm enough to sit on a bench in the courtyard. She loved the university because as the sign read, it was big enough to accommodate, but small enough to appreciate. The lawns were plush and the Dogwood trees displayed pink and white blooms. The tepid breeze felt invigorating as it blew through her hair. North Georgia resembled a scene from a postcard. She couldn't imagine a more beautiful place in the spring.

Annie opened her Sociology book. "Let's try this again," she whispered. There was something about the clean, crisp air that allowed her mind to absorb the words. After reading the chapters, she pushed her sleeve up to look at her watch. She still had an hour and forty-five minutes before Calculus.

She removed her notebook from her book bag and started answering the discussion questions.

"Excuse me," she heard a gentle voice say.

She looked up and felt her eyes widen. It was Dan.

"You're Angie?" he asked.

She smiled. "Annie."

His face turned red. "Sorry," he said. "May I?" he asked, nodding toward the bench.

"Sure, let me move my stuff," she said.

As he sat down, the breeze blew her long, pink sundress onto his pant leg. She tucked the excess fabric under her leg.

He smiled, as he nervously rubbed his hands together. "I hate to bother you, but I um kind of need some help," he said. Annie studied his expression, waiting for him to continue. He rubbed the back of his neck. "Would it be okay if I write down the questions Riley wants us to answer? Someone has torn page sixteen from my book," he said.

Annie smiled. "Yes, I just started working on the questions myself," she replied. "We can go to the library and make a copy if you would like."

"How many questions are there?" he asked.

"Five."

"Nah, I'll just jot them down if you don't mind."

She handed him the book and watched as he wrote down the questions. He had very neat handwriting for a guy.

"I don't get this one," he said.

"Which one?"

"Number two," he said, as he pointed at the page.

She leaned closer to him to read the question. "I think it's subjective. Not really a right or wrong answer," she said.

He bit the corner of his lip and shook his head as if he agreed. She could tell he still didn't understand.

"This is how I answered it," she said.

Just as she turned her tablet to show him, the wind blew the pages to where she had scribbled his name the night before. She slapped the pages back down and held the edge firmly with her thumb. She closed her eyes as she felt a wave of heat move from her neck into her face. Her heart began to pound so rapidly that she felt like it would come right out of her chest. She couldn't remember ever feeling this embarrassed. Last night she dreamed about running into him and now she wanted him to go away.

How could I be so stupid? she thought.

"That's a good perception of the inner-self," he said, pretending not to notice what had just happened.

This didn't make her feel any less embarrassed. He handed her the book and she could feel his eyes on her, but she was too mortified to look up.

"Thanks, Annie. I was beginning to panic because I didn't recognize anyone else from class."

Although, she was still in shock, she forced herself to smile. "Not a problem," she said.

As he stood up, she started to feel relieved.

"Okay, well...I'll see you tomorrow," he said.

****

"You didn't!" Kim shrieked.

Annie nodded. "Ohhh, I would rather die than go to class tomorrow," Annie whined.

"It's no big deal, Annie. So he saw his name in your notebook. What's so bad about that?"

It's a very big deal, Kim," Annie answered sarcastically. "How would you feel if you liked some...?" Annie gulped, wishing she could retract those words, but it was too late.

Kim's eyes widened. "You like him, huh?" she asked.

"NO! That's not what I meant."

"Annie, it's okay if you do. It's about time. Tell me again what he looks like," Kim said.

"Oh, I don't remember."

"Yeah, right," Kim joked.

"Look, I have to go," Annie said, feeling embarrassed that she brought up the subject.

Kim was being too presumptuous and Annie didn't feel like listening to the "You're going to have to give someone a chance" lecture again. She had no interest in Dan Wilson. She merely scribbled his name in her notepad because she was bored. It could have been anyone's name.

CHAPTER FOUR

"This is going to be the longest eight weeks of my life," Annie whispered, as she opened her closet and removed a pink floral skirt and denim jacket. It was her favorite outfit and she like the way it made her fee. She dreaded going to class so it was important that she felt confident. *Maybe he didn't see the notepad.* She tried to rationalize the situation since she always had a tendency to over analyze things. She placed her finger against her temple as she visualized the lip print surrounding his name. *He would have been blind not to see it.*

Kim and Dan were already seated at the table when she entered the room. Annie focused on Kim as she walked toward the back of the room, pretending not to notice Dan.

"Where were you?" Kim asked.

"Talking to Mark," Annie said, as she projected her voice. She wanted to make sure she said it loud enough for Dan to hear. She didn't want him to think she liked him and this would surely clear up any misconceptions. Kim raised her eyebrows as she glanced between Annie and Dan. She knew Annie too well and knew exactly what she was doing.

Mr. Riley walked into the room and placed his cup of tea on the edge of his desk. "Let's get started," he said.

From the corner of her eye, Annie could see Dan running his fingers through his hair. She loved the scent of his cologne. She wished she knew what he was thinking.

"The Assignment," Mr. Riley said, as he forced the chalk to form a thick, white line under the two words. "I trust that you have read the chapters and answered the discussion questions," he said.

Thanks for bringing this up, Annie thought. If it weren't for those discussion questions, she wouldn't feel so uncomfortable sitting next to the guy she couldn't stop thinking about. Not realizing that she was tapping her nails against the table, she could feel Dan and Kim staring at her. "Sorry," she whispered.

She was too nervous to look at Dan and wondered what he was thinking. Mr. Riley's lecture was very stimulating and it confirmed which profession she would choose. Prior to Annie's junior year, she narrowed her choice down to either teaching or social work. The latter choice was becoming more appealing.

Mr. Riley looked around the room. "Class...you will notice that I have written two words on the board. Look at these words carefully because in a few minutes, you will choose a packet that will explain the assignment in detail. You will be assigned a partner and the two of you will be expected to work together to analyzes and observe your case study," he explained.

The word partners caught everyone's attention as they looked around the room, wondering which person they would be assigned.

Mr. Riley continued. "What's a case study you ask? It will be some form of community work and you will have eight weeks to complete the assignment. At the end of the eight weeks, you will be asked to turn in a fifty-page composition, answering the questions in your packet. It would behoove you to take this seriously because the assignment will count toward seventy-five percent of your grade," Mr. Riley cautioned. His words of warning made it an exciting, but intimidating project.

"Maybe we'll be partners," Kim said. Annie shook her head in anticipation, as he called out names.

"Kim Taylor and Darren Matthews," Mr. Riley announced.

It was too late. Kim was assigned with Darren, Dahlonega University's star basketball player. Annie studied the faces of her classmates as some appeared to be happy with their partners and others seemed to be disappointed.

Mr. Riley continued. "Annie Carver and Dan Wilson." Their names seemed to be magnified as it echoed across the room.

NO! This can't be happening, she thought. *Please God, anyone but Dan.* Annie felt her stomach tighten.

Kim snickered, as she discretely tapped Annie's leg. Annie refused to make eye contact and stared straight ahead.

"Class, please make sure someone from each group takes a packet on the way out. You may want exchange phone numbers with your partner since you will be working so closely," Mr. Riley said.

"Lucky me," Annie whispered, sarcastically.

Kim winked. "It will be good for you."

Annie rolled her eyes, knowing that Kim found pleasure in this. "Well, I don't think this is one bit amusing," Annie said, as she walked toward the front of the room.

"Pick a good one," Dan said.

"Excuse me?" Annie asked in a confused tone.

He smiled. "The packet...pick a good one."

She felt his breath on her neck as he peered over her shoulder. They both reached for the large envelope and she tried to ignore the awkward feeling of his hand brushing against hers.

"Sorry, ladies first," he said, as he released his grip.

The sound of the bell caused chaos as students rushed from the classroom. "Quick, give me your number," Dan said. There was no time to retrieve a piece of paper. He traced her number on the palm of his hand as she blurted the numbers in sheer panic. She didn't wait for his response. Instead, she turned and ran down the hall.

****

Later that evening, Annie sat on the edge of her bed, staring at the yellow envelope. She couldn't quite grasp the concept of working with Dan. *Why him?* How would she ever survive eight weeks with him?

"Annie!" Jack exclaimed, as he opened her bedroom door.

"DAD!"

"How can you study with that music blaring?"

"It helps me block out all distractions."

It was evident by the look on his face that he found this hard to believe. "Well, I knocked but it's no wonder you didn't hear me. Do me a favor and turn it down a notch…or make that ten notches," he said.

"Okay, okay," she agreed.

"What's in the yellow envelope?" he asked, nodding toward her bed.

She sighed. "Oh, it's my assignment for Sociology class. Mr. Riley assigned us partners for a project," she explained. "It's supposed to count as seventy-five percent of our grade."

Her father crossed his arms and stared at the floor. "I wish your mother could be here to see how well you're doing. She would be so proud."

Annie felt a lump in her throat. "She knows, Dad."

He walked to the side of her bed and sat down. "Annie, I know I probably don't tell you as much as I should, but I'm very proud of you."

"Dad!"

"No, let me finish. Your mother and I used to stare at you in your crib and dream about what you would become. You have exceeded every dream and expectation that we...I ever had."

Her eyes clouded with tears. "I learned from the best," she said.

He smiled and shook his head. "Don't stay up too late," he said.

"Love you, Daddy," she whispered, as she patted his hand.

"Love you too, sweetheart," he said, as he closed the door.

She could hear silence before he turned to walk down the hall.

Annie stared at the envelope, wondering what was inside. *Maybe it was an assignment to work with underprivileged kids or homeless people.* She picked up the packet and ran her fingers across the silver clip. "No, I can't open it without Dan. I'll just have to wait," she whispered. The sound of the phone startled her, as she was deep in thought. She reached for the phone, but refrained from picking it up on the first ring. She didn't want to seem too eager to talk to him.

"Hello."

"Oh, my gosh. Can you believe who Riley paired me with?" Kim boasted.

"Oh, it's you," Annie said.

"Well, that's a nice greeting," Kim remarked.

"No, I didn't mean it that way. I was just hoping..."

"Oh, I know what you were hoping," Kim interrupted. "You thought it would be Dan," she said in a playful tone.

"Well...he is supposed to call to discuss the assignment, but I don't know if he'll call tonight," Annie said.

"Yeah, I know what you mean. I broke my neck to get home early in case Darren calls, but he hasn't yet. You know guys can be so irresponsible sometimes. I mean they say they're going to call and they don't, but we're always so naïve and wait by the phone," Kim whined.

Annie sighed as she listened to Kim rant and rave about the differences between men and women.

"Annie, you know I have always wanted to talk to Darren, but he seemed so unapproachable."

"Is that his name?" Annie asked.

"Like you didn't know," she said.

"No, I really didn't."

"Hang on a sec, got another call," Kim interrupted.

Annie waited for what seemed like an eternity before Kim realized she was holding on the other line.

"Oh my gosh, Annie. It's him. I'll talk to you tomorrow," Kim said.

Annie glanced at the clock. It was nine-thirty. She rolled onto her stomach and flipped through a beauty magazine. Thirty minutes had passed, but no call. Annie tossed the magazine toward the dresser, but missed. She sighed as she watched her mail scatter across the floor. She wasn't going to stay up all night waiting for Dan Wilson to call. He was probably on the phone talking to some gorgeous girl. She was sure the assignment was the last thing on his mind.

Annie sat in front of the vanity and brushed through her tangled hair. She gathered her hair into a French-twist and studied her profile from both sides before letting her hair fall down her back. She smiled as she thought about the time she would be spending with Dan. She initially perceived their partnership as a curse, but he intrigued her. *Oh, well, he'll have to call soon. Our grade depends on it.*

She curled into bed and turned off her lamp. Visions of his face plagued her mind as she replayed their conversation in the hall. Soon she surrendered to a deep sleep.

****

The sound of the phone startled her. After the third ring, she realized she wasn't dreaming. She glanced at the clock. It was ten forty-five. Barely coherent, she answered.

"Annie," a gentle male voice spoke. "Did I wake you?"

Her heart raced as she struggled to speak. "No...I mean that's okay," she groaned.

"I'm sorry. I didn't realize what time it was." He paused. "I didn't want you to think I forgot about the assignment."

"No, really it's fine. I'm glad you called."

"Really?" he asked.

"Yes, really."

There was silence and it was obvious they were both at a loss for words.

Dan cleared his throat. "Do you want to get together over the weekend? I know it's short notice and if you're busy, I'll understand," he said.

Trying not to appear too anxious, she disguised her excitement by waiting a few seconds to respond. "Actually, Saturday would work. I have plans on Friday night and church on Sunday," she explained.

"Do you go to church every Sunday?" he asked.

She hesitated for a moment. "Yep, Kim and I always go together. You know Kim from class, right?"

"You mean the boisterous blond who sits beside you?"

Annie laughed. "Yep, that's her."

"So you and Kim must really be close then?" he asked.

"Yes, she's my best friend." *Either he's extremely inquisitive or he's interested in Kim. Go figure.*

There was silence again. Annie twirled the phone cord around her fingers, wondering if she should say something, but nothing came to mind.

"Well, Saturday should work for me too since you're busy on Sunday. Oh and tell Mark not to get you home too late Friday night," he said with a chuckle.

Surprised by his remark, she became embarrassed, realizing he noticed her dramatic outburst in class. She remained quiet, not knowing how to respond.

Feeling awkward for making an unprecedented remark, he laughed. "It was a joke, Annie. I was teasing."

"Oh...funny," she laughed. *Was he really teasing?*

"Well, I better let you go so you can get your beauty sleep. I'll call you on Saturday morning and we can decide on a time to meet," he said.

No, please don't hang up. "Sounds good," she said.

After they hung up, she lay there, wondering what he was thinking. She pulled the pillow close to her and smiled as she thought about him mentioning Mark. *Did he really care?* She had a difficult time drifting to sleep. She imagined what it would be like to be his girlfriend. They would talk on the phone every night and go on real dates. *Dates that had nothing to do with the assignment.* He would put his arm around her and make her feel safe. She imagined their first kiss and how it would feel to fall in love. *Wait a minute! What was happening here? This wasn't like her. Could Dan Wilson really be making her feel this way?*

CHAPTER FIVE

❧

On Friday evening, Kim blew the horn as she pulled into Annie's driveway. They had plans to eat then catch a movie. After they confirmed the times for the movie, they decided to grab a pizza and make the eight-fifteen show. It was a warm night and they agreed it would be quicker to sit on the patio than wait for a table inside. Antonio's Pizza was a busy place, especially on weekends. Everyone loved the atmosphere and the pizzas were one of a kind.

Annie scraped the toppings off the pizza and pushed them to the side of her plate. She didn't have much of an appetite. All she could think about was Dan.

"Annie, what's wrong?" Kim asked.

"Nothing...why?"

"You keep looking at your watch. We have plenty of time before the movie, so just chill out," Kim said.

"I know. I'm sorry. It's just...well, never mind," Annie said.

"No, tell me. What is it?"

"Nothing, really."

"Come on, Annie. I can tell when something is bothering you. It's like you don't want to be here," Kim remarked.

Annie sighed. "Really, it's nothing. I'm just nervous about tomorrow, that's all."

Why are you nervous?" Kim asked.

Annie shrugged her shoulders. "I don't know...I just hope I don't say anything dumb."

Kim tilted her head and smiled. "You're not going to say anything dumb. Besides, it's not like a date.

Ouch! Annie lowered her brows. It wasn't what Kim said that disturbed her, but the way she said it. "Is it so hard to believe that someone of Dan's caliber could ever date someone like me?"

Kim winced. "Annie, I didn't mean it like that. I meant that you're getting together to talk about the assignment. You have no reason to feel intimated. If anything he should feel intimidated to be assigned with such a braniac," she said.

Annie forced a smile. She knew deep down that Kim wouldn't say anything malicious.

The remainder of the evening lingered slowly. Annie was anxious to get home in case Dan called. Even though he said he wouldn't call until Saturday, she was hopeful that he would. She regretted not telling him the truth about Mark.

She checked the answering machine when she got home, but there was only one message from her Aunt Susan. Annie fixed a glass of ice water then tiptoed upstairs to her bedroom, careful not to wake her father. After changing into her pajamas, she perused her closet for something to wear the next day. She couldn't make up her mind since she didn't know when or where they would meet.

She looked at the clock and wondered if it would be too late to call Dan. His number appeared on the caller identification, but she felt uneasy about initiating the call. She sat on the edge of her bed and picked up the phone. As she pressed the button, she hesitated before putting the receiver down. Annie tried to think of an excuse to call. *Tell him that something came up in the evening and you have to meet earlier*, she thought. No, that wouldn't be good because she wanted to spend as much time with him as possible.

She picked up the receiver again then looked at the clock. It was eleven. Convincing herself that it was too late to call, she curled into bed. *What am I thinking? He's probably out on a date with some cheerleader. Why am I doing this to myself?* As she pulled the pillow close to her chest, she whispered, "Dan Wilson."

CHAPTER SIX

It wasn't the sun peeking through the divide in the curtains that woke Annie; it was the sound of the birds chirping in the tree outside her bedroom window. She could feel the warmth of the air through the partially opened window. She rolled over to look at the clock. It was eight-thirty. She wondered what time Dan would call. Annie could hear her father in the kitchen. He wasn't exactly quiet, which made it difficult to sleep late on weekends. He worked at the hardware store on Saturdays. Annie arched her back and stretched her arms above her head. She usually went downstairs to tell her father goodbye before curling up on the couch to watch television. She always looked forward to Saturdays because it was the only day that she could be lazy.

Annie's father was pouring coffee into his thermos when she entered the kitchen. "Did I wake you?" he asked.

Annie smirked. He asked her that every week, but she never had the heart to tell him the truth. "No, I was awake. I'm meeting a friend today," she said in a cheerful tone.

Glancing over the top of his glasses, he continued pouring the coffee. "Do I know this friend?" he asked.

Annie smiled, but hesitated. "No, he's a guy from class. He's my partner for the Sociology assignment I told you about."

He studied her expression before placing the creamer back on the shelf. "Well, don't be too late tonight. You know I don't like you going out with people I don't know," he said.

Annie smiled. Her father was overly protective at times, but she appreciated his concern. "I'll be home early," she replied.

After her father left, she poured a bowl of cereal and flipped through the channels. Most channels were plagued with cartoons and infomercials. After finishing her breakfast, she made her way upstairs to take a shower. Not wanting to miss his call, she placed the phone on the shelf next to the shower.

After showering, she applied a generous amount of vanilla sugar lotion over her arms and legs. The fragrance always made her feel ultra-feminine. Annie wrapped a towel around her head and slipped into her robe. As she sat on her bed, she stared at the folder that contained their assignment. She wished the envelope wasn't sealed so she could peek inside. The clock on the nightstand indicated that it was nine-thirty. Just as she positioned herself in front of the vanity, the phone rang. Her heart raced. She couldn't pick up on the first ring and seem too anxious so she waited until the third ring.

"Hello."

"Morning," he said, with a raspy voice.

"Did you just wake up?" she asked.

"Is it that obvious?" he asked.

She laughed under her breath. "Just a little."

"What time did you get up?" he asked.

"Eight-thirty."

"Eight-thirty!" he exclaimed.

"I know, I know, but around here, it's hard to sleep late. My Dad is not exactly quiet," she explained.

"Mmm... must be nice. It's completely opposite around here. I would welcome noise," he said.

She wondered what he meant, but didn't think it would be appropriate to ask.

"So, what's on the agenda today?" he asked.

"I was hoping you would have thought of something," she said.

"Well, I'm not the one from around here so I guess you'll have to decide."

She thought it was cute the way that he was leaving the decision up to her. "Just because I'm from Dahlonega doesn't mean I should decide," she said. "By the way, where did you move from?"

"Florida," he responded.

"Wow! That must have been a bummer moving from Florida," she remarked.

He didn't respond. Instead, he changed the subject. "I'll make a deal with you. I'll pick you up at eleven and that should give you plenty of time to decide," he said.

She looked at the clock. "And what if I don't come up with anything?" she teased.

"Well, then I guess we'll just hang out with your parents all day," he said.

Annie was silent. The thought never crossed her mind that she would have to tell Dan about her mother. Not yet anyway. She felt uncomfortable, but tried to disguise it. "Eleven sounds great," she said.

After she gave him directions to her house, she panicked. Since they didn't decide upon a place to go, she was at a loss as to what to wear. She was even more concerned about how she would tell him about her mother. She hoped this wouldn't come up yet, but she had to be prepared. *You should just initiate the conversation and get it over with.* No, she thought. That would put a damper on the conversation.

She slipped on a pair of pink Capri pants and her favorite white baby doll shirt that tied in the back. She gathered her long dark hair into a ponytail and secured it with a pink band.

Annie grabbed her purse and waited outside. It was a beautiful day and she hoped they would spend some time outdoors. As she paced back and forth on the porch, she rehearsed a greeting. She wondered if Dan was nervous too. She glanced at her watch. It was ten minutes until eleven. She decided to sit on the porch swing instead of looking anxious.

Her stomach filled with butterflies every time a car passed by her house. She twisted a strand of hair around her finger as she examined her reflection in the window. The roar of a loud engine caught her attention as she watched a red car turn down her street. She watched in anticipation as the car slowed at every house. From a distance, it looked like a corvette. Surely, he doesn't drive a vette.

As the car turned into her driveway, she felt numb. *How appropriate... Mr. Perfect drives a perfect car.* She walked toward the steps to greet him. He looked amazing. He was dressed in khaki pants and a bright, blue polo shirt that accentuated his blue eyes. They walked toward each other until they met at the porch steps.

He smiled. "Sorry, I'm late. I missed your street and had to turn around."

"That's okay," she said with a shy grin, "Sorry the directions weren't good."

"No, it was my fault. I was going too fast and didn't see the street sign."

They both smiled.

"Do you want to come in?" she asked.

"Sure."

As he followed her into the house, she felt ashamed. Annie's parents bought the house when she was two.

Although it was a nice two-story house with a large porch, Dahlonega had several new subdivisions that displayed more modern homes.

Dan walked over to the wall of pictures. "Is this you?" he asked, pointing to Annie's graduation picture.

"I'm afraid so," she remarked.

"You look so different," he said.

Embarrassed, she managed to force a smile.

"Do you have any brothers or sisters?" he asked.

"Nope, I'm an only child."

She watched him as he studied each picture.

"Is this your mom and dad?" he asked, pointing to the last picture her parents had taken.

Oh no, here we go. Remain calm. "Uh-huh," she said. Annie adored that picture of her parents. They had it taken at their last high school reunion.

"That's a great picture. They look really happy," he said.

She could feel her stomach tighten. "They are.... were....," she said in a melancholy tone.

He glanced at her then back at the picture. "Divorced?" he asked.

Annie was silent as she pondered how to answer the question.

He glanced back at her. "I'm sorry, it's really none of my business," he said.

"Mom passed away." *There. You said it. It's all out in the open now.*

Embarrassed, he turned from the pictures to catch a glimpse of her expression. "I'm so sorry," he said, "I....had no idea."

"It's okay; I like talking about her. It keeps her memory alive," she said.

His expression relaxed as he turned toward the pictures again. "Cute dog," he said.

"Yeah, that's Barney. He ran away a few years ago and we haven't seen him since," she explained.

Dan's eyes widened. "Maybe I should be quiet," he joked.

She laughed. "It's okay. Do you want to see the rest of the house?" she asked.

"After you," he said.

He followed her through every room, taking notice of the details of the architecture. "This is a nice house," he said.

"Thanks, it's old; but I love it."

"I love old homes. I wish we had one," he said.

Annie looked perplexed. "Where do you live?" she asked.

He was silent for a moment. "Gold Ridge Manor."

Annie's eyes widened. Gold Ridge Manor was a prestigious subdivision situated in the midst of an elaborate golf course. All of the houses listed for six-hundred-thousand dollars and above. She suddenly felt ashamed and began to question the sincerity of his compliments.

Dan glanced at her, wondering if she pegged him for a spoiled, rich kid. He regretted mentioning his subdivision. Crossing his arms, he leaned against the kitchen counter. "Well, what's the plan?" he asked.

Annie slowly lifted her gaze to his and shrugged her shoulders.

He grinned. "You don't know, do you?" he asked in a playful tone.

She smiled as she twirled a strand of hair through her fingers. They stood there in an awkward silence, smiling as they exchanged glances.

"How far is the lake from here?" he asked.

"Um, about a thirty minute drive," she responded.

He studied her expression, unable to tell if she was receptive to his idea.

"Are you hungry?" he asked.

"A little."

"Okay, well, let's grab a few sandwiches and head for the lake," he suggested.

Annie was surprised by his suggestion. "The lake?" she asked with a smile.

"Yeah, why not?" We can have a picnic and go over the assignment.

The lake, a picnic... how romantically uncomfortable. "Okay," she agreed.

"Oh, do you have an old blanket or something that we can sit on?" he asked.

Annie snapped her fingers. "Be back in a sec," she said.

When she returned with the blanket, he was staring at the pictures on the wall. She pretended not to notice. "Ready?" she asked.

"After you."

Annie made sure the front door locked behind her as she followed Dan to his car.

He opened the car door for her and made sure she was buckled before he backed out of the driveway.

"This is an awesome car," she said.

"You like it?" he asked.

He ran his fingers through his hair, just like he had done so many times in class. Annie smiled as she watched him change gears. She never had an opportunity to ride in a sports car before. She closed her eyes as the warm air from his window blew her hair away from her face.

"Too much wind?" he asked.

She smiled. "No, it feels good."

The drive to the lake was pleasant. They talked about everything from cars to the assignment. Annie felt more at ease than she imagined. She attributed this to the fact that he did most of the talking. She wanted to ask him about Florida, but it was obvious he didn't want to talk about it.

Annie speculated that he probably had a girlfriend and was bitter about moving.

"Do you have any brothers or sisters?" Annie asked.

He shot a quick glance her way then looked away. "An older sister," he remarked.

When they arrived at the lake, they found a shaded spot that was perfect for a picnic. The sound of boats and children's laughter provided a lively atmosphere. Dan opened the bag of gourmet sandwiches and handed one to Annie. They were anxious to learn about the assignment and decided to eat their dessert later.

"Well, shall we end the suspense?" he asked.

Annie nodded as she handed him the envelope.

"Oh, you're going to give me the honors?" he asked.

He took a sip of iced tea, then slowly opened the envelope. Annie watched his face in anticipation. His forehead wrinkled as he glanced between her and the document.

"Well, what is it?" she asked.

He handed her the paper.

Annie read the words aloud.

"Congratulations on your first journey into social work. You and your partner have been assigned the opportunity to work with an elderly widow in the community. She will be your case study. You will be expected to meet with her at least twice per week to fully engage in the understanding of social patterns of the elderly. The packet consists of eight questionnaires, one for each week. Please call the number at the bottom of the form to obtain the name and address of your case study. Good luck to you."
Regards,

Mr. Riley

Annie looked at Dan. He was staring at a young boy tossing bread to five hungry ducks.

"What do you think?" Annie asked.

Dan shrugged his shoulders. "I don't know. I guess I'm just..."

Before he could finish, Annie interrupted. "Disappointed?" she asked.

He smiled. "You too, huh?"

Annie tucked a loose strand of hair behind her ear. "I was just hoping to get a more exciting assignment. Teenagers or children would have been really cool," she said, in a discontented tone.

They turned their attention to the boy feeding the ducks.

"Kids are so innocent. The least little thing amuses them," Annie remarked.

Dan laughed. "Yeah, look at how much fun he's having with those ducks. What I would give to be his age again. Everything is new and exciting."

The boy started crying as his father patiently explained that they didn't have any more bread.

"Hey, do you have any bread crumbs left?" Annie asked.

"Huh?" Dan asked.

"Do you have any bread crumbs from your sandwich?" Annie asked.

Dan opened the sandwich wrapper. "No, just a pickle," he said.

Annie chuckled. "Well, I don't think the ducks would appreciate a pickle.

Dan smiled as he watched Annie crumble the wrapper. He couldn't take his eyes off her. She looked beautiful with the wind blowing through her long ponytail. Most of the girls in Florida kept their hair short. She felt his stare, but looked away, hoping he would do the same.

"I wonder what she's like." Annie said.

Confused, Dan raised his eyebrows. "Who?"

Annie nodded toward the paper. "The elderly lady. I wonder if she's nice."

He shrugged his shoulders.

She could tell that he didn't have much interest in the assignment. "How many questions do we have to answer for the first analysis?" Annie asked.

Dan flipped through the pages until he found the first section. "Thirty," he said.

"Thirty!"she exclaimed. "Do they look difficult?"

He stared at the page and frowned. "Immensely."

Annie bit the corner of her lip as she listened to Dan read some of the questions. The assignment seemed more difficult than she had imagined.

"Is it too late to change our major?" she joked.

He laughed. "Don't you wish?"

His smile gave way to a serious expression as he admired her beauty. She nervously rubbed the back of her neck. *Okay you can look away now.*

He sensed her discomfort and looked through the questionnaire, trying to refocus on the reason they were there. "We have to read two chapters and review assessment number one before we meet with her," he said.

Annie wrinkled her nose. "Well, that doesn't give us much time,"she said.

He smiled. "Not to mention finding time to study for our other classes," he said.

Dan held the bag of cookies in front of Annie.

She nodded. "No, thank you."

His mouth dropped. "You're going to pass up double chocolate fudge cookies?" he asked.

Smiling, she nodded. She loved his sense of humor. He had the personality to match his good looks. She felt guilty about judging him based upon her first impression. He wasn't snobby at all; considering, he lived in a mansion.

"How do you want to do this?" he asked.

"Do what?" she asked.

He held up his finger as he quickly chewed. "Do you want to meet after class a couple of days before we meet with her?"

Annie laughed. "You mean you're going to trust me to coordinate this?" she asked.

He smiled as he gave her a subtle wink. "Yeah, you're right. Maybe I should plan this," he joked.

She felt butterflies in her stomach as she looked into his blue eyes. She never knew anyone with such captivating eyes. His were deep blue with a hint of violet.

They were silent as they watched the boats race across the water. Annie wanted to savor every moment of the day. She enjoyed Dan's company and loved the mere thought of being on a picnic with him, even if it wasn't a real date. In all the years that she had been to the lake, she had never been on a picnic.

Dan stretched out on his side with one arm supporting his posture. "Well, what's it going to be Miss Annie," he asked.

She smiled and shrugged.

"You're busy tomorrow with church, right?" he asked.

She nodded.

"How about Monday night?" he asked.

"That would be great," she said. *Monday couldn't arrive soon enough.*

"Can we study at your house?" he asked.

She nodded. "Yes, then we can study at your house the next time," she said.

His forehead wrinkled as he looked away. "You don't want to come to my house," he said, in a solemn tone.

"Yes, I do," Annie remarked.

His face displayed a serious expression. "I would rather not," he said.

Annie gave him a quizzical look. She knew there was something mysterious about his home life, but he wasn't comfortable enough with her to talk about it. Why would he be?

"We can just study at my house, but I'm warning you that my Dad will talk your ear off," she said.

Dan smiled. "I think I can handle that," he said.

****

It was seven o'clock and people were starting to pack up and leave. The park transformed from such a lively atmosphere to a calm, desolate place in such a short amount of time. Annie knew they would have to leave soon. The drive back to Dahlonega was serene as they savored the warm air passing through the windows.

Annie's Dad was sitting on the front porch when they pulled into the driveway.

"I guess it wouldn't be a good time to give you a goodbye kiss," Dan joked.

Her eyes widened as she felt the blood rush to her face. *Okay, take a deep breath, he was just joking.* "Well, thanks for the picnic," she said.

"You're welcome. I had a good time," he remarked.

They sat there in silence for what felt like eternity. "Well, let me walk you to the door," he said.

Annie bit the corner of her lip as she glanced at her father's silhouette sitting in the rocking chair. "Are you sure?" she asked.

Dan looked into her eyes. "Would you rather I not?" he asked.

"No, of course not. I didn't want you to feel obligated since my father is there," she answered.

With his arm resting on the steering wheel, Dan tilted his head. "Annie, I would never dream of dropping a lady off without walking her to the door," he said.

She studied the sincerity in his eyes.

"Wait here," he said, as he gently patted her knee. He walked around to the passenger side and opened her door.

She felt nervous as they made their way toward the porch. "Hi! Daddy," she said in a nervous tone. "This is Dan. He's my Sociology partner," she explained.

Annie's father stood up and extended his hand. "Nice to meet you, Dan. I'm Jack."

"Thank you, sir; it's nice to meet you too," Dan responded.

Annie's father gestured toward the swing. "Would you like to sit down?" he asked. Annie felt anxious about her father talking to Dan.

"Thank you.... sir."

Annie was amazed at how calm and comfortable Dan felt with her father. She was the one who felt unnerved. After all, she had never brought a guy home before. Well, that wasn't necessarily true. There was the senior prom when she agreed to go with Mark, but only as friends. It was obvious her father liked Dan.

"That's a nice car you have there, son," Jack replied.

"Thank you, sir."

"What year?" Jack asked.

"98."

"It's a beauty," Jack replied.

Dan nodded. "I appreciate that, sir."

Annie's father waved his hands. "Please...,call me Jack," he insisted.

Dan smiled. "You're welcome to look at it, Jack."

Annie glanced at her father. His fatigued face transformed into a bright gleam. She couldn't recall the last time he smiled. Annie remained seated on the swing while they walked toward the car. She smiled as she daydreamed about being at the lake with Dan. She could hear her father and Dan talking, but paid little attention to what they were saying. She was too entranced with the memories of the day.

"Annie," her father called.

The sound of his voice quickly brought her mind back to reality.

"We're going to take it for a spin around the block," he said.

Dan handed the keys to her father. *He's almost too good to be true.* Her father hesitated, but Dan persuaded him to get into the driver's seat. Dan smiled at her as he got into the car. She waved as they backed out of the driveway.

Annie was elated to see her father so happy, but at the same time, she longed for them to hurry back. She wondered what they were talking about and hoped her father wouldn't boast about her too much. He had a tendency to do that with anyone who would listen. Annie knew she was her father's whole world and he was everything to her too.

She heard the sound of the loud motor as the car turned down her street. Her heart began to pound faster. She hoped he would stay for a while.

"Miss us?" Dan asked, with a sheepish grin.

"Immensely," she joked.

Dan smiled at Jack. "You should have seen your father. He went from zero to sixty in three seconds."

Annie glanced at her father who was beaming again. He smiled as he patted Dan on the back. "I appreciate your kindness, son. I used to dream about having a vette."

"Well it's never too late, Jack," Dan responded.

Annie's father laughed. "Maybe someday, but for now, I'll just keep my old truck."

Dan flashed a humble smile at her father.

The last hint of daylight dissipated and with darkness, came a slight chill.

"Well, kids, I'm going to turn in. It's been a long day and this tired, old body needs to recharge," he said.

"It was nice meeting you, Jack," Dan said, as he extended his hand again.

"Ah, the pleasure was all mine. You were very kind to allow this old man to fulfill one of his dreams," he said, with extreme sincerity.

Annie kissed her father on the cheek. "Goodnight, Daddy."

As he closed the screen door, her heart began to accelerate. She could feel her palms getting sweaty as she remembered his comment about giving her a goodnight kiss. *I feel faint. I think I'm going to pass out.* She took a deep breath as she made her way across the porch. He looked so good in the moonlight.

"Do you want to go inside?" she asked.

He shook his head. "I would rather sit out here...., if that's okay."

Great! You would say that, wouldn't you? "Okay," she agreed.

Dan motioned for her to sit beside him on the swing. "Are you cold?" he asked.

Uh, no. I'm actually feeling feverish. "I'm fine," she answered.

They sat there in silence before either one of them spoke a word. She knew she should say something, but her mind went blank. Just as she mumbled the first word, Dan began to speak.

They laughed. "Go ahead," he said.

"No, you first," she responded nervously.

"I insist," he said.

Annie cupped her hands together. "I was just going to thank you again for today. I had a great time."

Dan smiled as he stared into her eyes. She glanced away, pretending not to notice. She wanted more than anything to look at him, but his stare made her feel uncomfortable. *Chicken. Look at him.*

He sensed her discomfort and gently elbowed her. "Well, I better go and let you get some sleep since you have church tomorrow."

Annie didn't want him to leave, but she didn't want to appear too anxious by asking him to stay.

"Does your father go to church with you?" he asked.

Annie shook her head. "No. Not since mom passed away," she whispered.

Dan nodded. "How does he deal with it?"

Annie sighed. "I honestly don't know. People deal with things differently, but for me, I find solace in my faith and going to church. Dad likes to stay busy and be alone," she explained. Dan leaned forward and cupped his hands between his knees. "Yeah, faith is sometimes the only thing you can count on," he said.

It wasn't what he said that piqued Annie's curiosity, but it was the way he said it. Dan had a mysterious side to him. He didn't want to disclose anything about his personal life. She didn't know why, but hoped he would eventually open up to her.

"Well, I better go," he said.

Annie smiled as she walked with him to the edge of the porch. "Thanks again for everything," she said. He squeezed her shoulder and smiled. "It was fun." She nodded as she forced herself to look into his eyes.

"Sleep well," he whispered.

"You too," she said.

She watched him as he walked to his car. He opened the car door and paused before getting in. "Talk to you on Monday?" he asked.

"Yeah," she answered. She wanted to tell him to call her after church, but she couldn't find the nerve. Instead, she watched him drive away until his taillights could no longer be seen.

CHAPTER SEVEN

Annie described every detail of the lake to Kim as they sat on the pew and watched the people congregating before the service.

"I tried calling you last night, but couldn't get you," Annie said.

"I'm sorry. I left my cell phone in Darren's car and didn't realize it until after I got home." Kim covered her mouth to disguise an unexpected yawn. "I didn't get home until after midnight," she whispered. "By that time it was too late to call."

Annie and Kim continued whispering, as they made their way to the choir. The sound of the piano forced them to stop. "We'll talk more after church," Kim said.

Annie's mind began to wander during the sermon, as the pastor talked about how people should refrain from judging others. Annie felt guilty for judging Dan, based upon her first impression. There was no doubt his family had money, but he was down to earth. She thought about how kind he was to her father and how his actions were genuine. She was so disappointed with herself for not asking him to call her after church. Now, she would have to wait until the next day to see him. She looked up. *Would it be wrong to pray for a call?*

After the service, Kim and Annie stood in the parking lot, talking for half an hour. Of course, Kim bragged that her evening was more of a date than a forced assembly. Annie stood with her arms crossed as Kim described every aspect of the evening. Darren took her to the movies, then to a nice dinner before they went back to his house and talked to his parents. Annie was anxious to tell Kim more about Dan, but she waited patiently for her turn.

"So, tell me more about the lake," Kim said, with a suggestive grin.

Annie smiled, shaking her head. "I know what you're thinking and it's not like that. We had a good time, but..."

"But what?" Kim asked.

Annie paused for a moment. "There's one thing that bothers me about him."

"Well," Kim said, with an expression that begged for more details.

"He's so secretive about his home life," Annie explained. "Oh, and are you ready for this? He lives in Gold Ridge Manor."

Kim's eyes widened. "Gold Ridge Manor! Are you kidding me?"

"No, but he's not proud of it, either," Annie said.

Dismissing the serious tone in Annie's voice, Kim laughed. "Well, when you tour his palatial palace, I want to go too."

Annie shook her head. "Oh, I don't foresee that happening. He made it crystal clear that he didn't want me to see his house."

Kim shot a quizzical look. "That's strange."

"Oh, by the way, tell me about your assignment," Annie said.

Kim explained that she and Darren would have to meet with a troubled teen that had gotten mixed up with drugs and alcohol. Annie's eyebrows arched as she listened to Kim.

"I'm hoping to bring her to church sometime," Kim said.

"How old is she?" Annie asked.

Kim shrugged her shoulders. "I'm not sure yet, but the paperwork implied that she's a very young teen."

"Oh, you're so lucky. You have my...our dream assignment," Annie said.

Kim shielded her eyes from the sun. "Yeah, we'll see what a dream it turns out to be," she said. It was obvious that Kim and Darren had a more challenging assignment than Annie and Dan's case study.

Kim reached into her purse for her keys. "Well, I better go. Darren is picking me up later," Kim said.

As Kim drove away, Annie thought about driving through Gold Ridge Manor to see if she noticed Dan's car in any of the driveways. She was intrigued by the subdivision, but even more fascinated with him. Annie almost convinced herself to drive through his neighborhood, but she feared his reaction. Would he be mad?

Annie decided to take the long route home and look for his car. She remembered that Gold Ridge Manor had a security gate and she wouldn't be able to enter. She drove by slowly, hoping that he would exit through the gate. Unfortunately, she didn't see anyone entering or leaving. Annie decided it was a ridiculous idea and turned around.

She was disappointed, but knew she shouldn't call him. Although, his number still appeared on the caller id, he never asked her to call. She would have to go home and find something to occupy her time until the next day. Maybe by some small chance he would call. Annie knew this probably wouldn't happen. She came to terms with the fact that the remainder of the day would be uneventful. She would go home, change clothes, and sit on the front porch and read some beauty magazines.

After she turned down her street, she noticed a red car in her driveway. Her eyes widened. "It can't be," she whispered.

As she pulled into the driveway, she saw her father and Dan sitting on the front porch. They were looking at a book or something, but it was hard to determine what it was. Annie took a deep breath before she got out of her car and walked onto the porch. *Remain calm and play it cool.* Her father was showing Dan pictures from some old photo albums. "Wow! What a surprise to find you here," Annie said.

Dan smiled as he held up her sunglasses. "You left these in my car," he said.

"Thanks. I wondered what I did with them, but….. you didn't have to make a special trip," she said.

Dan's face turned red. "I had to run some errands anyway, so it was no big deal," he said.

"I'm showing Dan some old pictures," her father explained.

Gee, thanks, Dad. She smiled. "So I see." Annie sat in the rocking chair and watched as her father explained each picture to Dan. She found it ironic that a few minutes earlier, she was driving by his part of town and he was at her house.

Annie's father gathered the photo albums and politely excused himself, before going inside.

Now that they were alone, Dan flashed a shy smile as he studied her expression. It was evident he was embarrassed. He cleared his throat. "You look really nice," he said.

"Thanks," she responded. "How long have you been here?"

"About half an hour. I…. have to be going soon, but wanted to return these," he explained, handing her the sunglasses.

Annie wasn't sure how to respond. She wanted to ask him to stay, but didn't know if he was being sincere in wanting to return the glasses and leave. Just as she was about to speak, her father opened the screen door. "Dan, do you have plans for dinner?"

Annie's eyes widened in disbelief. Dan glanced at her, trying to determine what she was thinking. He wasn't sure if she wanted him to stay. After all, she had told him she wouldn't be able to get together until Monday. He shifted in the swing, reluctant to respond.

Please stay. No, don't stay. I mean, oh, what do I mean? Annie looked at Dan, anxiously waiting for a response.

"Um, no, but I don't want to impose," he responded. "Annie probably has plans."

Annie glanced between her father and Dan before speaking. "No, I don't have any plans today," she said.

"Good. It's settled," her father said. "I'll grill some steaks and Annie can make the potatoes and salad. My daughter makes the best loaded baked potatoes," her father bragged.

Annie looked embarrassed. "Daaaaddd," she said, in a sarcastic tone.

Her father smiled at Dan. "She hates when I brag about her."

Dan chuckled, as he studied Annie's expression. He still couldn't determine if she wanted him there, but he knew one thing. He had a strong yearning to be near her.

Knowing it would be several hours before he had to start dinner, Annie's father went back inside to take his usual Sunday afternoon nap. Annie remained in the rocker, twirling her pearl bracelet around her wrist, as she struggled to find the right words. Dan appeared to be having the same problem. Finally, the silence became too awkward for him and he turned to look at Annie. He gave her a slight smile before speaking. "I wish you wouldn't talk so much," he said, jokingly.

Annie chuckled. He had such a good sense of humor and always knew the right things to say. "Yeah, you talk a lot yourself," she said.

He smiled as he stared into her eyes.

"Why are you looking at me like that?" she asked.

"I usually look at people when I have a conversation with them," he said, as he raised his eyebrows.

Annie tilted her head and gave him a sarcastic smile. She hated when they were at a loss for words. "I'm going to go inside and change clothes. Do you want to wait in the living room or out here?" she asked.

"I like it out here," he said.

"Ok, I'll be right back," she said.

Annie removed her jewelry and neatly placed each piece in her armoire, as she thought about spending another day with Dan. She slipped on a pair of denim shorts and a white T-shirt. After getting dressed, she pulled her hair into a pony-tail and dabbed on some lip-gloss.

When she went back downstairs, she could hear Dan arguing with someone through the screen. She peeked through the curtains and could see him talking on his cell phone. He was standing with his back toward the front door. He had one hand grasping the back of his hair, as he shook his head. She walked closer to the screen door to listen. "Take the car, I don't care," he said. Annie knew he must have been talking with one of his parents. She quickly stepped back from the window, as he turned around. She decided to wait a few minutes before walking outside. She didn't want it to be obvious she heard the conversation.

Annie went into the kitchen and poured two glasses of iced tea. When she returned to the front porch, Dan was sitting on the swing. His face was red and she knew he was upset. "I thought you might be thirsty," she said, handing him a glass.

"Thanks," he said as he took a sip.

Annie sat down beside him. She could tell he was frustrated, but she refrained from asking what happened. "I'm glad you're staying for dinner," she said.

"Yeah, me too," he said. His entire demeanor had changed and she wished she knew the right thing to say.

"Hey, do you want to start reading the chapters today?" she asked.

He shrugged his shoulders. "Sure, why not?" he responded.

Annie went inside to retrieve her Sociology book. She wanted to do something to help Dan take his mind off the conversation he had with his parents. As she sat down beside him, she moved a little closer so they could share the book. "I'll read one chapter and you can read the next," she said.

From her peripheral vision, she could see Dan's eyes, as they shifted between her and the book. Annie never thought of herself as being pretty, but she wondered if he thought differently.

Annie read one chapter then handed the book to Dan. She listened closely while he read the words. She loved the way he talked. Everything about him was perfect. After he read the chapter, he handed the book to Annie.

"Do you want to go ahead and review the assessment while this is fresh in our minds?" she asked.

He shrugged, as he crossed his arms in front of him. "Yeah, sure."

They discussed the correlation between the chapters and their case. It was more difficult than they imagined because they hadn't met with the elderly lady yet. The assessment was designed to analyze what they anticipated would happen during the first meeting. Once the meeting took place, they would have to compare what they expected versus what transpired.

Annie was having a harder time grasping the assessment than Dan. This frustrated her since she never had problems from an academic standpoint. She wondered if he was getting frustrated with her.

"I'm sorry, Dan. This stuff usually comes so easily for me, but I can't seem to figure this out. I hate being defeated," she admitted.

He playfully elbowed her. "You're not defeated. Look, don't think of it that way. It's difficult to predict what is going to take place. We haven't even met her," he said.

Annie didn't look convinced. She ran her fingers down the rusty chain that secured the swing.

Dan sensed her frustration. "Remember when you helped me with the questions?" he asked.

Ahh, the infamous day when the wind blew the pages to where his name was scribbled in her notebook. She nodded.

"I was confused, but you told me the answer was subjective, and there was no right or wrong answer. It's the same principle here," he said, trying to convince her.

Her train of thought was broken when her father opened the screen door. "You kids getting hungry?" he asked.

Annie looked at her watch. "I can't believe it's five thirty," she said. "Yes, I'm more than ready to put this aside for a while," she said.

Dan smiled, as he walked toward the door. "Need some help, Jack?"

Annie's father motioned for Dan to follow him. "You can keep me company while I grill the steaks if you'd like."

Annie watched them through the window, as she prepared the salad and baked potatoes. It was nice having someone else at the dinner table. She could tell that her father was ecstatic to have company as well. She inspected the worn dishes and decided to use the china that her mother loved to use for special occasions.

After they sat down, Annie motioned for her father to say the blessing. He cleared his throat and thanked the Lord for the food and their guest. He was never one to prolong a prayer.

"So, Annie tells me you moved from Florida. How do you like it here so far?" Jack asked, as he spread butter across a piece of bread.

Annie's throat tightened, as she shot a quick glance toward Dan. She hoped that he wouldn't feel uncomfortable by her father's question.

Dan wiped the corner of his mouth with a napkin and nodded. "I like it," he responded. Not wanting to elaborate, he quickly changed the subject and complimented Annie's father on the flavor of the steak. "And the potatoes are out of this world, too," Dan said, as he winked at Annie.

She blushed, but smiled. In an effort to deter her father from asking more questions, she began telling him about their assignment.

After dinner, Dan helped Annie clear the table, while her father went outside to clean the grill. As she turned around to wipe the table, he bumped into her. He extended his arms to prevent her from hitting her head on his chest, but they accidentally embraced.

"Sorry," she said, meeting his gaze. He rubbed her arms gently, as she backed away. He knew he made her nervous and this bothered him. He wanted her to feel comfortable around him, and he tried to use his sense of humor to lighten the mood. "You could have killed me with those salad tongs," he said.

She flashed a nervous smile. "You're quite the comedian, aren't you?"

He gave a sheepish shrug. "Hey, do you want to finish the assessment?" he asked.

Annie frowned. "I guess we should. Do you think we could meet her tomorrow or Tuesday?" Annie asked.

"Maybe," Dan said, following her to the front porch.

As they took their familiar places on the swing, Dan moved closer to Annie. Not wanting to appear too obvious, she discretely eased over, allowing more room between them. He pretended to be oblivious to her actions.

"Did I tell you about Kim and Darren's assignment?" Annie asked.

He shook his head. "No. What?"

"They get to work with a troubled teen. I think she had an addiction to drugs or alcohol," Annie explained.

Dan curled his fingers under the swing, as he leaned forward. "Now why couldn't we have gotten an assignment like that?" he asked.

Annie sighed, as she turned toward him. "Remember me telling you my mom passed away?"

Shocked by the sudden change in subject, Dan shifted his eyes to Annie. "Yes," he said.

"She was killed by a drunk driver. I hate alcohol and drugs. I hate irresponsible people, who are so selfish, that they don't consider the consequences of their actions," Annie blurted out.

Dan studied her face, as it transformed into a mournful expression. "Annie," Dan whispered, "I...I don't know what to say. I'm so sorry."

Annie glanced into his eyes. "No, I'm sorry. I don't know why I just told you that," she explained.

He gently patted her hand. "I'm glad you did," he said.

Annie stared straight ahead. "It's strange. I was initially envious of Kim and Darren's assignment, but I don't think I could have handled it. It would have been a little too close for comfort," Annie said.

"Yeah, I know what you mean," he agreed.

They continued reading and discussing the assignment, until the pink sky surrendered itself to shades of gray. The streetlights began to come on, one by one. Annie's father said goodnight to Dan, before he retired to his bedroom for the night.

"Well, it's getting late and I should go," Dan said.

Annie felt guilty for confiding in Dan, about her mother. It had been a nice day and this was how it was going to end. "Thanks again for coming over and helping me with the assignment. I know Dad really enjoyed having you here."

He looked at her, wondering if she enjoyed his company, too.

She sighed. "I hope I didn't make you feel uncomfortable, because."

Before she could finish her sentence, Dan playfully elbowed her. "Hey, please don't apologize. I'm glad you told me, and you didn't make me feel uncomfortable."

Not completely convinced, she just nodded.

It took everything in him to refrain from hugging her. "Well, I better be going, but I really had a great time today. Tell your Dad thanks again for dinner," he said.

"I will," she said.

They stood there in silence, looking at each other, just like they had done the night before.

"See you tomorrow?" Dan asked.

Annie smiled, as she nodded. "Yeah, see you tomorrow."

****

Annie was dying to tell Kim about spending another day with Dan. As she dialed Kim's number, she stared out her bedroom window. The streets were dark, and although there was little traffic on her street, she continued peering out the window. She would give anything to see him again.

"Hello," Kim answered.

"Hey, it's me. You're not going to believe who was at my house when I got home from church," Annie said.

"Who?" Kim asked.

"Dan!" Annie exclaimed.

"No way! But I thought...."

"I know, but I left my glasses in his car, and he was nice enough to bring them by," Annie explained.

"Wow! He must really like you to make such a special trip," Kim said.

Annie laughed. "No, it's not like that. He had to run errands, so it wasn't like it was out of his way."

Kim snickered. "Oh, Annie. Get a clue! He wanted to see you or he would have waited until tomorrow," Kim said.

Annie wished that was true, but refused to believe it. She assumed he wanted to drop her glasses off and leave, but felt obligated to stay since her father insisted. "He stayed for dinner and we worked on our assignment."

"Mmmhmm. You like him, don't you?" Kim asked.

Annie tried to downplay the situation. "Only as a friend," she answered.

Kim snickered. "Yeah, that's why you sounded like you won a million dollars," she said.

Why don't you just admit it to her? "Well, I'm glad he came by, because Dad enjoyed his company," Annie said defensively.

Kim laughed. "Okay, I won't put you on the spot now, but only because I need to go. Darren's getting ready to leave," Kim said.

"Oh, I'm sorry. I didn't know he was still there. We can just talk tomorrow," Annie said.

"Ok, I'll talk to you tomorrow," Kim said.

Annie changed into her pajamas and adjusted the pillows on her bed, to support a comfortable reading position. She removed the assessment from the folder and stared at the answers Dan had written. Why was she having a difficult time understanding the questions? She never had this problem before. He had a way of making her lose her train of thought. She felt embarrassed for confiding in him about her mother. Annie put the folder aside and turned off her lamp. After an hour of tossing and turning, she drifted to sleep.

CHAPTER EIGHT

"Annie, wait up!" Dan yelled. She turned around and watched him as he made his way through the crowded hallway. She felt her heart beat faster as he moved closer.

"Morning," he said, breathlessly.

She felt a wave of shyness again. "Morning," she said, with a smile.

"Listen, I don't have much time, but I wanted to ask you if you still planned on us getting together this afternoon?" he asked.

Are you kidding? That's all I have thought about since you left last night. "Yeah, that's fine," she responded. "Are we going to meet her today?"

Dan smiled. "You're anxious, aren't you?" Annie curled her lips, as she shrugged her shoulders.

He knew she was more excited about meeting the elderly lady than he was. "Let me see what I can do to arrange it. I'll make the call in between classes," he said.

Annie stared into his deep, blue eyes and nodded. She trusted that he would coordinate the visit. Although she was eager to meet their case study, she longed to spend more time with Dan.

The sound of the bell created a chaotic scene as students scrambled in every direction.

"I'll come by your house around 5:30," he said.

"Sounds good," she responded.

"Later, Annie."

She loved the way he said her name and hoped the day would go by fast.

****

Annie was writing her father a note, when Dan knocked on the door. She peeked around the corner and could see him through the screen. "Come in. I'm just letting Daddy know that I won't be home until later," she said.

Dan waited in the hall while Annie finished the note. He looked away from the pictures when she entered the hallway.

"I'm ready. What's she like? What time can we meet her?" Annie asked.

He laughed. "Wow! Aren't you the inquisitive one?"

Annie tilted her head to the side and gave him a playful smile. "Of course, I'm curious. This is important," she said.

Dan raised his eyebrows and gave her a sheepish grin.

"Come on, tell me. Please," she pleaded.

"Ok, ok...., I don't know,... 6:30," he answered.

Annie frowned. "You didn't actually talk to her, did you?" she asked.

"No, the social worker said she would schedule it, but we'll find out all about her tonight," Dan said. "Speaking of..., we better get going, so we have plenty of time to find her house." Dan handed the directions to Annie and told her to navigate, since she was familiar with Dahlonega.

Neither of them spoke much, other than to discuss the directions. As they turned onto a side street, adjacent to the historical part of Dahlonega, Dan slowed down to read the numbers on the mailboxes. "Well, it looks like this is it," he said, as he pulled into the driveway.

Annie stared at the house in amazement. It was an old, white Victorian house with an immaculate lawn. The flowerbeds were full of pink and white impatiens. The porch displayed white wicker furniture with floral cushions. It was evident the lady was wealthy. Annie looked at Dan, who seemed to be less than impressed by the grandeur. She knew he had plenty of money, and material things didn't seem to impress him. He seemed embarrassed by his wealth.

"Shall we?" he asked.

Annie bit the corner of her lip. "I'm kind of nervous," she confessed.

Dan gave her a comforting wink. "We'll be fine," he said.

Not completely convinced, Annie hesitated, before opening the car door.

They walked to the front entrance and paused before ringing the doorbell. They could see a distorted figure walking toward them, but it was difficult to see through the frosted glass. Annie's heart began to beat faster, as the squeaky door reminded her of something out of a horror movie.

As the door opened, their case study was finally revealed. She was a small-framed woman, probably in her late seventies, with a slight hunch. She was nothing like they had expected. The elderly lady wore black pants with a red silk shirt. The top button was secured with a diamond broach. Her short, white hair was cut in a bob-type style. She wore a subtle hint of make-up, but very natural looking. Annie thought she was a very striking woman, who was probably very beautiful in her younger days.

"You must be the students they told me about," she said. Her tone was barely cordial. She didn't exude any excitement in having them inside her home.

Dan smiled. "Yes, I'm Dan and this is Annie."

The elderly lady glanced at Dan, but focused her attention on Annie. She looked her up and down. "I'm Mrs. Hildebrand," she said.

Annie extended her hand. "We're very pleased to....,"

Before Annie could finish the sentence, the elderly lady motioned for them to step inside. "Come in and do so quickly. The flies have been horrible," she said.

Dan looked at Annie and although he didn't say anything, she knew what he was thinking. They followed Mrs. Hildebrand into the large foyer.

"We will visit in the parlor," she said.

As they walked into the parlor, Annie looked around the room in amazement. She remembered the round-shaped room when they pulled into the driveway. The room contained a very high ceiling with ornate crown molding. The red, Oriental rug covered most of the hardwood floor, but it was easy to see the floor was still in good shape. Oversized cherry furniture and massive paintings made the room look like something in a decorating magazine.

"Would you care to partake of some hot tea?" Mrs. Hildebrand asked.

"None for me," Dan said, wrinkling his nose.

Annie was embarrassed by his tone. "No thank you, Mrs. Hildebrand. You have a beautiful home," Annie said.

The elderly lady tossed her head back. "Yes, I've been very happy with it. Please sit down," she said, as she motioned toward the large white couch.

They watched the elderly lady, as she slowly lowered herself into a burgundy Queen Anne chair, adjacent to the couch. Dan and Annie sat down simultaneously. Without saying a word, Mrs. Hildebrand stared at them. As they exchanged glances, Annie leaned forward, crossing her arms as if she were cold.

Dan cleared his throat. "Have you lived here for a long time?" he asked.

Her long, bony fingers stroked the broach. "Forty-two years," she answered sternly. Annie smiled. "Wow, that's a long time. You must have lots of memories in this house." Mrs. Hildebrand nodded. "I do."

Dan raised his eyebrows and gave Annie a slight smile. It was an awkward conversation, as the lady was brief with her answers. This was going to be more difficult than they anticipated.

Annie reached for the folder she had placed beside her. "Mrs. Hildebrand, I assume you are aware of why we are here," Annie said.

"I am," she responded coldly.

Annie lowered her head and pretended to look at the questionnaire. Dan knew Annie was at a loss for words. The elderly lady wasn't making it easy for them. He felt compelled to take over. "Mrs. Hildebrand, we um.... We are enrolled in a sophomore Sociology class and our assignment is to meet with you and..."

Before he could finish the sentence, Mrs. Hildebrand interrupted. "Young man, I'm well aware of why you are here."

Refusing to be intimidated, Dan leaned forward, returning the cold stare she was giving. "Then I..., we assumed you agreed to this," he said.

Annie felt her stomach tighten into a knot. Mrs. Hildebrand wasn't the sweet, grandmotherly person Annie had envisioned. Their grade required them to spend time with the elderly lady, no matter what the cost.

Annie cupped her hands together as she prepared to sweet talk the lady. "Yes, as Dan was saying, we have to complete the assignment, and we are really looking forward to spending the next couple of months getting to know you."

"Yeah, right," Dan mumbled under his breath.

Annie's eyes widened as she pretended not to hear his comment.

Mrs. Hildebrand continued stroking her broach. "I will afford you the opportunity to write about my lifestyle and you will in return, assist me with some minor things that need to be done around here," she scowled.

Annie nodded. "Yes, ma'am, that's correct."

Mrs. Hildebrand made a movement with her index finger. "Very well, shall we proceed? I like to follow a schedule because I usually retire every night around nine o'clock," she said.

It was apparent that Mrs. Hildebrand was educated. She was well spoken and her grammar was impeccable.

Mrs. Hildebrand turned around to look at the clock, as if she mentally set a timer. Dan snickered. Refusing to look at him, Annie gave him a slight poke with her elbow. He smiled, but stared straight ahead.

Annie searched her purse for a pen. As she flipped through the pages of the questionnaire, Dan moved closer to her. Their arms were now touching. Annie shot him a nervous glance. He sensed her discomfort and motioned his head toward the questionnaire. He wanted her to believe there was a purpose for sitting so close. *What do I have to do to make her comfortable with me?*

Annie glanced at the clock and gave a quick smile at Mrs. Hildebrand. "Okay, question number one asks you to describe the most memorable time of your life," Annie said.

They looked up in anticipation of what she would say. Mrs. Hildebrand tucked a strand of hair behind her ear. Annie's eyes were focused on the magnificent ring on the lady's right hand. It was a pear-shaped diamond that must have been at least three carats.

"Well, let me see," she said, resting her index finger on her cheek and nodding. "I would say my early thirties."

Dan and Annie looked at each other with disappointment. Annie held the pen still in her hand. "Yes, I'm sure that was a very nice time, Mrs. Hildebrand, but could you elaborate on a specific event or something memorable?" Annie asked.

Mrs. Hildebrand rolled her eyes and sighed. "My dear, I just told you my early thirties was the most memorable time in my life. If I elaborated on everything, you would be here more than two months, now wouldn't you?" she asked.

Dan leaned closer to Annie. "Just write down her early thirties and we'll beef it up later," he whispered.

Annie nodded. She pretended to study the next question, while she mustered up the courage to proceed. "Okay, question number two asks if you would describe your present life as equally, more, or less content, than the time you described in question number one."

Mrs. Hildebrand sighed. "Well, if you ask me, that's a rather preposterous question, don't you think?"

Annie scratched the back of her head and looked at Dan for guidance.

He cupped his hands together and leaned forward, focusing all of his attention on Mrs. Hildebrand. "Ma'am, with all due respect, we don't understand what you mean by preposterous," he said.

Mrs. Hildebrand slowly straightened her posture in the chair and crossed her arms. "Young man, what I mean is the questions contradict each other. I told you the most memorable time in my life was when I was in my mid-thirties. This should be a good indication that no other time, including the present, could compare to that period in my life," she retorted.

Dan leaned back and rubbed his hands on his legs. "Understood..., but would you say that you are happy for the most part, now?"

Refusing to make eye contact with Mrs. Hildebrand, Annie focused her attention on the planks on the floor. She admired Dan for his persistence in gathering the information.

Mrs. Hildebrand waved her hand at Dan. "Yes, yes, just write down that I'm overwhelmed with happiness."

Shaking his head, he snickered.

Mrs. Hildebrand didn't find his sarcasm amusing. "Well, it's been a rather long day and I'm fatigued," she said.

Annie offered another smile, as she cleared her throat. "Well, we don't want to overstay our welcome, but we certainly appreciate your time."

Mrs. Hildebrand stood. "I'll walk you to the door," she said.

Dan and Annie followed her into the entrance of the house. "Would it be an intrusion if we met with you again this week?" Dan asked.

Annie admired his courage, but tensed, in anticipation of Mrs. Hildebrand's response.

With her back to them, she shook her head. "Tomorrow isn't good for me, but perhaps you could return on Wednesday evening around five-thirty. I will prepare a list of duties I need done, in exchange for my time with your little project," she said.

"List of duties?" Dan asked.

Annie discretely elbowed him, hoping the lady wouldn't notice.

"Yes, the list of duties. You didn't think there would be no reciprocation, did you?" she asked.

"No ma'am; we will be here on Wednesday evening to assist you in any way we can," Annie said.

Mrs. Hildebrand opened the door and closed it before they were down the steps.

"Geez, what's her deal?" Dan asked.

Before Annie could respond, he gave a sarcastic chuckle. "I can't wait to see this list of duties," he said.

Annie smiled, as he opened her car door. She was disappointed with the visit, but hoped the next visit would prove to be more productive.

"She's going to be a challenge," Annie said, buckling her seatbelt.

"Yeah, but she'll definitely be an interesting challenge."

"Did you see the size of that ring on her finger?" Annie asked.

Dan laughed. "No, I didn't pay any attention," he said.

Annie giggled. "I don't know how you could have missed it," she said.

They continued talking about the assignment, and how much they dreaded the next two months.

As they pulled into Annie's driveway, Dan's cell phone rang. He looked at the phone and pushed the ignore button.

"You don't need to take the call?" Annie asked.

"Nope," Dan said.

"Well what if it was important?" Annie asked.

Not wanting to have this discussion and spoil the evening, he relied on his levity to lighten the mood. "More important than the list of duties?" he asked, disguising his voice to sound like Mrs. Hildebrand.

Annie laughed. "Dan you're awful….funny, but awful."

Dan shut off the engine and glanced at her house, before focusing his attention on her. A hint of moonlight allowed him to see her dark hair glistening against the window. She was so beautiful, so innocent. *I'm not ready for the night to end, he thought. Quick, think of a reason to prolong the evening.* If possible, he would have moved Heaven and Earth to steal another hour with her.

"Hey, I know it's getting late, but would you like to grab a quick bite to eat?" he asked.

Annie looked at him, but this time she didn't break the stare. His blue eyes were so mesmerizing and this made it too difficult to look away. He slowly reached for her hand

and began to rub it. Just as their hands locked together, his phone rang again. He released his grip and reached for the phone. It rang four times, before transferring to voicemail. "Amazing," he whispered, as he threw his head against the back of the seat.

Annie studied his expression. "Maybe you should get that."

"No, it's fine," he said, staring straight ahead.

Annie looked confused. "Dan, come on. What's going on?" she asked. *It had to be a girl.. a girlfriend.*

"Annie, you worry too much. It's nothing…, trust me," he said.

Annie felt a lump in her throat as she tried to swallow. *Why am I getting so upset? Don't let him know you care.* She gave him a sympathetic smile. "Maybe we should take a rain check and go to dinner another night," she suggested.

No. Please. It took everything in him to refrain from begging her not to go inside. Dan sighed as he stared out the window. "Okay," he said in a whisper.

As they walked to her door, neither of them spoke a word. Annie was disappointed with the way they were ending the night. She found it hard to believe that just a few minutes before, they were practically holding hands. The mood was different now.

As they reached the door, Dan squeezed her shoulder. "Are you okay?" he asked. Without making eye contact, Annie nodded, but she wasn't convincing. He closed his eyes for a moment, wishing he had turned off his phone. All of his efforts to get close to her were blown. *How could I be so stupid?* he thought.

Tilting his head to force her to look into his eyes, he whispered her name. She faked a smile. "Are you sure you're okay? You seem miles away," he said.

She yawned, pretending to be tired. It was true, she was hurt. She had disclosed everything about her life, yet his personal life was secretive and off limits. "I'm sorry," she said, "I'm just tired and disappointed with Mrs. Hildebrand. That's all….really."

Dan stared into her eyes, not knowing if she was being honest. He didn't want to make her feel uncomfortable and decided he should say goodnight. "Well, I better let you get some rest," he whispered.

Annie flashed another fake smile. "Yeah, I'll see you in class tomorrow," she said.

She remained on the porch until his taillights could no longer be seen. She pulled her hand toward her nose, savoring the scent of his cologne that remained on her hand.

She took a deep breath before making her way into the house. As she sat in front of her vanity, she stared at her reflection. Did he see her the way she perceived herself? Did he like her? She tried to analyze the situation. Would he have tried to hold her hand if he didn't like her? But what about the phone calls? Did he have a girlfriend? *What's wrong with you? Why are you letting this guy get to you?* She closed her eyes, trying to erase the chaos from her mind. As she curled into bed, she tried to focus on their next meeting with Mrs. Hildebrand.

CHAPTER NINE

Annie and Kim decided to eat lunch in the courtyard, since it was such a beautiful day. The lawn was packed with students eating on blankets, and every bench in the courtyard was occupied. Annie noticed one group of students throwing food to a stray cat. They watched in anticipation to see if the cat would surrender and move in close enough to eat the food.

"That reminds me of Jill," Kim said, in a solemn voice.

Annie looked confused. "Excuse me?"

Without taking her eyes off the cat, Kim continued. "That cat…. It reminds me of Jill, my case study. She wants to trust people, but she's afraid."

"So tell me, how did your meeting go?" Annie asked.

Kim shrugged her shoulders. "I don't know, Annie. It's hard to explain. I mean, Darren and I knew Jill had a drug addiction, but this is a lot more difficult than we thought it would be."

"Yeah, I guess Riley's really putting us to the test," Annie said. "Our meeting was no picnic, either."

Kim continued telling Annie about the meeting with Jill. "Darren is so good with her, but she's so confused. "What do you think about me inviting her to church on Sunday?"

Annie nodded. "I think it's a great idea. We have a lot of teenagers, and who knows, she may really like it."

Kim shifted her attention away from the cat and turned toward Annie. "So, what happened with your meeting?"

Annie crossed her arms. "That old..... I mean, Mrs. Hildebrand is going to cause us to fail. I just know it."

Kim's mouth dropped. "Annie, I'm shocked. I've never heard you say a cross word about anyone."

Annie smirked. "Yeah, well, she isn't the sweet, old lady that I envisioned. She was mean and rude."

Kim offered a consoling look. "That bad, huh?" she asked.

Annie rolled her eyes. "You couldn't even imagine. Dan's right. Mrs. Hildebrand is only doing this to get free labor around her house."

Kim laughed. "Well, like you said, Riley is trying to give us a flavor for what a career in social work or psychology would be like. Besides, I'm taking advantage of spending time with Darren. I'm finding out we have a lot of things in common."

Annie's mind wandered, as Kim described her evening with Darren.

"Hey, listen to me go on and on," Kim said. "How are things going with Dan?"

Annie shrugged one shoulder and hesitated before answering. "He's sweet and funny, but it's just like I told you, he has this mysterious side to him. We were sitting in his car last night and his phone rang, but he wouldn't answer it. It's just weird," Annie explained.

Kim looked perplexed. "What's so weird about that?" she asked.

Annie looked irritated at Kim's response. "Come on, Kim. Would you just sit there and ignore your phone if someone tried to call you? Twice," she added.

Kim shrugged her shoulders nonchalantly. "Maybe it was another girl and he didn't want to be rude and take the call with you sitting there."

With those words, Annie felt a lump in her throat. Even though she suspected this, it was difficult to hear from another point of view. It was the only logical explanation though.

"Annie, are you okay?" Kim asked. "You have this weird look on your face. Annie had a difficult time hiding her feelings. Her facial expressions revealed the truth.

Kim squinted her eyes, focusing on Annie's expression. "Ooohhh, my gosh," she said, nodding slowly."

Annie shrugged. "What?"

Cupping her hand over her mouth and removing it slowly, Kim flashed a sympathetic smile. "You're falling for him," she said.

Annie shook her head. "No, I'm not!" she exclaimed defensively.

Kim sighed. "Annie, I've known you forever, and until now, no guy has ever rattled you. You can be honest…."

Before she could finish, Annie interrupted. "He's not rattling me, I assure you. I was merely telling you about something I found to be rather mysterious. He's just my study partner."

"Okay, okay," Kim said, holding her hands up.

Annie decided not to tell Kim about Dan rubbing her hand. If she misunderstood his gesture, she would risk being embarrassed. She wished she wouldn't have to face Dan in class, but she had no choice.

****

Annie barely spoke to Dan before class and he could sense something was wrong. It was extremely difficult to concentrate on Riley's dissertation, but she pretended to listen. She could feel Dan's eyes on her, but refused to look his way. She knew she had no right to be upset with him. They didn't know each other well enough to have feelings…

but she did. She loved being near him, but felt like a fool for misunderstanding his gesture.

The sound of the bell was a relief. She could go home, spend some quality time with her father, and forget about the day. As she gathered her books from the table, she dropped her keys.

Dan leaned over. "I'll get them," he said.

Annie held out her hand to take the keys, but he smiled, as he played tug of war. "I'll walk you to your car," he said. This was not what Annie wanted. She didn't feel like playing games with him, and she certainly didn't want him to walk her to the car. Dan tried to make small talk about class, but Annie said very little. As they reached her car, Annie held out her hand again to retrieve the keys. "Please," she said.

Dan smiled. "Under one condition."

Annie sighed. "What condition?"

"You have to ride to the lake with me," he said.

Annie looked confused. "The lake?" she asked.

Dan nodded. "Yes, it's that large body of water we went to last Saturday," he joked.

She tried desperately not to laugh. "I don't know, Dan, I have to..."

"Please," he interrupted.

Annie stared into his eyes. *How can I say no when you look at me like that?* "When?" she asked.

"Now," he answered.

"It's already four-thirty," she said, trying to offer an excuse.

"So, it's four-thirty," he said. "It doesn't get dark until eight-thirty or nine. Please, it's really important," he urged.

She sighed again. "Why the lake?"

Dan leaned closer to her. "I like it there," he whispered.

Annie stepped back, forcing more room between them. She didn't want to misunderstand his actions again, but she felt so drawn to him.

"But my car is here," she said.

Dan glanced at her car. "I'll follow you to your house and we'll go from there," he said.

Annie periodically glanced in the rear view mirror, and wondered why he wanted to go to the lake. Moreover, why did he want her to go if he had a girlfriend?

As they drove to the lake, Annie thought about different ways she could approach the subject of his having a girlfriend. She had to handle the situation with a degree of finesse. She didn't feel comfortable enough to ask point blank, but she was determined to find a way to bring up the subject.

Although it was late afternoon, the lake was crowded. The parking lot was full with trucks and boat trailers. Dan guided Annie to the edge of the water. "It's so peaceful here," he said. Annie watched the expression on his face, as he stared at the water. She hoped he would feel relaxed enough for her to bring up the girlfriend subject.

"Let's go over there and sit," he said, pointing to a picnic table. They sat side by side on the table, and watched the boats racing through the water.

"That looks like it would be a blast," Annie said.

"Do you like boats?" he asked.

Annie smiled as she pointed to a small speedboat. "I would love to be on that one right now," she said.

Dan chuckled. "That's a fast one," he said.

They walked around the park, watching boats and engaging in small talk for two hours. Although, she enjoyed spending time with him, she wondered why he made such a big deal out of going to the lake.

"Let's go back there," he said, pointing to the picnic table.

Annie glanced at her watch. It was almost eight o'clock. People were starting to pack up and leave. They sat on top of the picnic table, as they watched the last boat being pulled from the water. "Do you think we should head back?" Annie asked.

Dan chuckled. "Is that your subtle way of saying you're tired of my company?"

"No, not at all," she said. I just meant it's getting late and we have to meet with Mrs. Hildebrand tomorrow. God knows it's going to be a long day," she laughed.

Dan leaned forward, rubbing his knees, and glancing into her eyes. "Annie, before we leave, can I ask you a question?"

Oh no. Why does he sound so serious? "Ok," she said.

Dan cleared his throat and hesitated. "Did I?. I mean, were you? Oh, man..... How do I ask this?"

Annie turned to look at him, not knowing what he was trying to ask. "What?" she asked.

His face turned red, as he hesitated again. "Did I make you feel uncomfortable last night, you know, when our hands touched?"

Annie felt her heart beating rapidly. *Did he mean to do this?* Maybe she didn't misread his actions. She didn't know how to answer the question, but knew she had to say something. "Um, no." I.... wasn't sure if you meant to," she said.

Dan flashed a shy grin. "Well....Did you want me to mean it?" he asked.

Talk about putting me on the spot. This was a question she had to answer carefully. If she said yes and he didn't mean anything by it, she would feel like a fool.

Without breaking her stare from the water, Annie decided to play it safe and turn it around on him. "Was it intentional?"

He chuckled nervously, knowing she didn't want to answer the question. "Yes, I meant it."

Annie felt her stomach fill with butterflies. "You did?" she asked, hesitantly.

He nodded. "I didn't know if you were upset with me. Everything seemed to be going great until then and now you just seem.....distant," he explained.

She didn't know what to say. He didn't get it. It had nothing to do with him holding her hand. She was elated that she didn't misunderstand his actions. How could he not know why she was upset?

"Annie, I'm sorry if I made you feel uncomfortable. I hope this doesn't make you regret working together on the assignment," he said.

Annie let out a deep breath. "Dan, it's not that," she said.

Surprised by her response, he studied her expression. "What is it then?" he asked.

Frustrated and embarrassed, Annie stared at the ground. She didn't want to answer the question. All of her intentions to trick him into disclosing whether the calls were from a girl went out the window. How could she tell him it bothered her and that she liked him? She had no right. He didn't make any promises to her. They were just study partners.

"Annie," he said.

She shook her head and continued looking at the ground. She knew she had to answer him, but this was such an awkward situation. Glancing at him then toward the lake, she shrugged her shoulders. "It's nothing, really," she said.

He knew she wasn't being honest and this bothered him, but he could sense her discomfort and decided to change the subject.

He cleared his throat. "I better get you home. Like you said, we have a long day tomorrow."

The drive home was uncomfortably quiet and this allowed Annie plenty of time to replay the conversation in her mind. Why couldn't she just open up and tell him what she wanted to? Why was it so difficult? She didn't want to end another night like this, but she just couldn't tell him.

Dan walked her to the door, just like he had done every time before. They glanced into each other's eyes and it was obvious there was so much to say, but neither of them attempted to make conversation.

The silence was too much for him. "Talk to you tomorrow?" he asked.

She nodded. She decided not to wait on the porch until he drove away. She was too frustrated. Annie opened the door and walked into the living room. Her father was sitting in his recliner, watching the news. She sat on the arm of his chair, engaging in small talk, before saying goodnight.

As she lay in bed, staring at the clock, she wished he would call. She was desperate to talk to him. It would have been much easier to talk to him on the phone than in person. As she tossed and turned, she replayed their conversation in her mind, until she slipped into a deep sleep.

CHAPTER TEN

The line at the Big Bear Café extended out the door. Students pointed to the menu display behind the counter, as they discussed the best deals. The sign read.

"Wednesday's special"
$5.99 for a sandwich, chips
or fries and a medium drink."

Annie and Kim looked around the café for an empty seat, but it was evident they were out of luck. They gathered their food and started walking toward the college. Dahlonega was a great college town because the campus was close to several fast food places.

As they walked back to campus, they decided to sit on a bench in the courtyard. Kim patted Annie's arm. "I'm really sorry for what I said yesterday. I didn't mean it."

Annie smiled. "I know, she paused, I wasn't completely honest with you."

Confused, Kim raised her eyebrows.

Glancing at her friend, Annie sighed. "I didn't tell you this, but Dan tried to hold my hand the other night."

Kim's mouth dropped open, as she pointed her finger at Annie. "I knew there was more to it," she said.

Annie shrugged. "Yeah, but then he apologized, because he thought it offended me."

Kim studied her friend's expression. "And did it?" she asked.

"No, but the phone calls are still a mystery," Annie explained.

Just as Annie was about to tell Kim what happened at the lake, Darren yelled across the lawn. "Oh, sorry Annie, I forgot I told Darren we would meet at 1:00 p.m. We'll talk later. Wish us luck with Jill," Kim said.

Later, when Annie drove home, she decided to take a detour by Dan's subdivision. She had always been fascinated with the landscaping that surrounded the golf course. The houses were nestled far from the road, but the enormous structures could be seen from a distance. She had hoped to catch a glimpse of Dan driving through the gates. No luck again, she thought. She would have to wait until later to see him.

Annie hoped Mrs. Hildebrand would be more hospitable than she was during the first visit. Although, she dreaded meeting with her again, she knew their first assignment had to be turned in the following week. Annie worried about not having enough substance for the paper, but Dan assured her they would enhance the answers.

As she looked through the papers and began making a rough draft, she glanced at the clock. Dan would be arriving shortly. She briefly glanced at the questions they were going to ask Mrs. Hildebrand.

Annie heard Dan's car pull into the driveway. She checked herself in the mirror and walked outside. As usual, Dan looked amazing. He was wearing blue jeans and a white polo shirt. She could smell the familiar scent of his cologne as he moved closer to her.

"Well, are we ready for round two?" he asked.

Annie laughed. "Hopefully, it won't be as brutal as the last one," she said.

"Yeah, let's hope not," he said.

When they pulled into Mrs. Hildebrand's driveway, they noticed a small figure in the garden. "Is that her?" Annie asked.

"I doubt it. I can't see her working in a garden," Dan said.

As the car approached the top of the driveway, they continued studying the frail figure and concluded it had to be her. Of course, she didn't offer to turn around and acknowledge them. They walked to the edge of the garden and watched her, as she sprayed water onto a yellow rose bush. "Hello, Mrs. Hildebrand," Annie said.

Without turning around, the elderly lady continued watering. "You have to be so careful with these," she said. "They are very delicate flowers. Too much water, not enough water, too much sunshine, not enough sunshine, can kill them in an instant," she explained.

Annie walked closer to the rose bush. "It's very beautiful. My mom would have loved it. She had a thing for yellow flowers," Annie said.

Standing with his arms crossed, Dan flashed a sincere smile.

Mrs. Hildebrand tugged at the water hose, but it was tangled around a large, clay pot. "You're speaking about your mother in past tense," Mrs. Hildebrand said.

Annie cleared her throat and inhaled sharply. "Yes ma'am. My mother passed away several years ago, but she loved yellow flowers. Actually, she loved anything yellow," Annie explained.

The lady turned her head to steal a quick glance at Annie. "I see. Shall we go inside?" she asked.

Dan and Annie followed her into the house. It was strange seeing her in casual attire. She was wearing khaki pants and a beige and pink floral shirt. It was different from the fancy clothes she had worn during the first visit. Mrs. Hildebrand motioned for them to take their familiar seats in the parlor.

Annie pulled the questionnaire from the folder and glanced at Dan. "Do you want to ask the questions?" Dan nodded his head toward the paper, indicating he wanted Annie to ask the questions. He edged closer to her, their legs almost touching.

Annie crossed her leg, forcing some distance between them. As she flipped to the first page of the questionnaire, she forced a hesitant smile at Mrs. Hildebrand. "Um, question number one asks you to describe your life as a young child," Annie said. They looked up at Mrs. Hildebrand, in anticipation of her answer.

Annie's eyes were drawn to the magnificent ring again. She couldn't stop looking at it. It was unlike the small stone her mother had worn. Annie hoped they would find out more about the elderly lady. She was eager to learn the story behind the ring, because it was no ordinary piece of jewelry that you would find in a mall store. It had to be personally designed for Mrs. Hildebrand.

"Mrs. Hildebrand," Dan said.

At the sound of Dan's voice, Annie quickly diverted her attention from the ring to the lady's face.

Mrs. Hildebrand had the same sour look she had during the first visit. "Define young child," she demanded.

Dan sighed and it was obvious that he had become frustrated. The elderly lady made no attempt to cooperate, and Annie knew if things didn't improve, they would fail the assignment. They were already faced with the challenge of having to embellish the answers to the first questionnaire.

"Mrs. Hildebrand, it doesn't really matter the age. The question didn't ask for a specific age, so if you could please just think back to your childhood and expound a little," Annie said.

Dan smirked as he crossed his arms. He was shocked that Annie took such a stern tone, but he was glad. Mrs. Hildebrand was trying his patience.

They both looked up to see how she would respond. "Well, okay. No need to get in a tizzy," Mrs. Hildebrand said.

Feeling guilty for being abrupt, Annie felt compelled to apologize. "I'm sorry, ma'am. I didn't mean to offend you, but this is important to us," Annie explained.

The elderly lady cocked her head to one side, as she raised her shoulders in an arrogant manner. "Nonsense, I wasn't offended. I simply asked a question for clarification purposes. It seems to me, you were the one who got upset, my dear."

*Upset? You think I'm upset? Why I'll show you....*just as Annie was about to speak, Dan felt the tension and decided to intervene. "Nobody is upset, Mrs. Hildebrand. We're just anxious to hear about your life," he said.

Mrs. Hildebrand smirked at Annie, then smiled and batted her eyelashes at Dan. "Young man, I'm not foolish enough to believe for one minute, that you are interested in my life. You and I both know why you're here," she said.

Annie leaned forward, trying to scrutinize the elderly lady's face for signs of anger. Why was she treating them with such disrespect? If she didn't want to assist with the assignment, why did she volunteer?

Annie swallowed hard, feeling anger and sadness. Mrs. Hildebrand obviously harbored pain and animosity. "Mrs. Hildebrand," Annie spoke softly. "It's true we're here to complete an assignment, but we're very interested in your life story. Dan and I were just talking the other night about how fascinating life must have been when you were growing up. I'm sure it was less chaotic."

Mrs. Hildebrand flashed a slight smile, as she examined her hands.

"Please, Mrs. Hildebrand," Annie pleaded. "Could you share some stories and paint us a picture of what it was like?"

The elderly lady cupped her frail hands together. "Very well," she said, as she glanced between Dan and Annie. "I was born in Memphis, Tennessee, and was one of five children—three brothers and one sister. My father moved us to West Virginia when I was.... oh, let me think about it. I was six or was it seven? Six I believe."

Annie wrote the words as fast as Mrs. Hildebrand spoke them. Dan glanced between the paper and Mrs. Hildebrand, making sure Annie didn't miss anything.

"He was a coal miner," Mrs. Hildebrand continued. "He had to go where there was work. I remember my poor mother having to break the news to her parents. We lived with my grandparents."

Mrs. Hildebrand raised her eyebrows. "Oh, I'm sure you're thinking it must have been a sight with all of us kids, but those were good times," she said, as she used her hands to enhance the story.

Dan and Annie smiled at each other, as Mrs. Hildebrand's face transformed into a peaceful expression. She clasped her hands together and rested her chin on her knuckles. "We didn't have much, but then again, nobody did. We didn't know we were poor," she continued.

It was hard for Annie to imagine Mrs. Hildebrand as being poor. She was so curious to learn more about her life and how she came into money. Annie and Dan became so enthralled with her story; it was hard to believe three hours had passed.

Annie placed the documents back into the envelope. "Well, Mrs. Hildebrand, we better let you get some rest, but we thoroughly enjoyed our visit," Annie said.

Mrs. Hildebrand nodded, as she pulled a piece of paper from a book that was lying on her table. "Here's the list of duties I would like for you to complete," she said. "Anytime this week would be sufficient."

Dan opened the folded piece of paper and read the items. Annie couldn't see the paper, but she could tell by the expression on Dan's face, that he was irritated.

"May I see?" Annie asked.

Dan handed the piece of paper to Annie. As she read the list, she tried to maintain a fake smile.

Repair and paint broken bird feeder
Stain three benches in the garden
Paint the mailbox
Plant impatiens
Clean china in the cabinet
Arrange box of pictures in photo album
Clean attic

This was more than a list; it was a full-time job. Annie couldn't believe Mrs. Hildebrand expected them to do all of these things, in exchange for participating in their project. It was clear to them they were being taken advantage of, but what choice did they have? They had to complete the assignment to pass the course.

As the elderly lady walked them to the door, she reiterated her desire to have them start on the chores immediately.

"We'll be in touch, Mrs. Hildebrand," Annie said.

As they walked to the car, Annie remained quiet. She could tell that Dan was not amused.

He rested his hand on the steering wheel, as he stared toward the house. "That old lady is going to be the death of me. I didn't realize we were going to have to practically live here," he said.

Annie couldn't help but laugh, as he complained and mocked Mrs. Hildebrand's voice.

As they pulled into Annie's driveway, she noticed her father peeking through the curtains. She knew he had a hard time going to bed without knowing she was home. Dan noticed this too. "Do you think he would mind if I said hello?"

Annie smiled. "No, he would probably like that very much."

As they walked into the house, Annie's father was sitting in his recliner, flipping through the channels. "Daddy, someone's here to see you," Annie said. Her father smiled when Dan walked into the living room.

"Hi, Jack. I hope you don't mind, but I asked Annie if I could come in and say hello," he said.

Jack smiled. It was evident he was delighted to see Dan again. "Noooo. You're always welcome here, son." He glanced at Annie. "How's your assignment going?"

Annie plopped down on the arm of her father's chair while Dan took a seat on the sofa.

Jack listened as they explained the difficulties they were encountering with Mrs. Hildebrand. "You wouldn't believe it, Daddy. She wants us to clean her attic, and paint, and plant flowers," Annie whined.

Her father laughed, as he patted her leg. "Well, sounds like you two have your work cut out for you," he said.

They continued laughing and talking until the ten o'clock news came on. Jack excused himself and went into his bedroom to watch the news.

Now that they were alone, Annie wondered if Dan would try to hold her hand again. Even though he admitted that holding her hand was intentional, she couldn't be entirely sure he had feelings for her. Their eyes followed her father, as he approached the last step, and turned to make his way down the hall. Annie glanced across the room at Dan. He smiled as he patted the cushion on the couch, motioning for her to sit beside him. As she made her way toward the couch, she looked toward the staircase. Although she was ecstatic to sit beside him, part of her wished her father would return, forgetting to program the coffee pot.

She slowly eased to the end of the couch and rubbed her hands together. Dan turned toward her, placing his elbow on the back of the couch. She glanced up and noticed he was staring at her. "What?" she asked.

He shook his head and smiled.

"What?" she asked again.

"I was just…" As he was about to finish his sentence, his phone beeped. It was obvious he silenced the ringer, but the beep was an indication he had a message.

Annie glanced at the phone, then at him.

Dan pretended not to hear the beep, as he continued looking into Annie's eyes.

She was annoyed and she could no longer hide it. "Dan, what's going on?" she asked.

He casually shrugged, as if not understanding her question.

"Why don't you ever answer your phone when you're with me?" she asked.

He lowered his brows. "What's wrong with you?" he asked, in a confused tone.

"Me? What's wrong with you?"

He looked away, not knowing how to respond.

Annie stood up. "Dan, why won't you answer me?" Her voice was shaking.

"I better go," he said, as he stood up.

It was all she could do to fight back the tears. "How long are you going to play this charade?" she asked.

Shaking his head, he stared at the floor.

Annie crossed her arms. "See, you refuse to answer me. Are you ashamed for someone to know you're with me? Or is it the fact you have a girlfriend?" She paused for a moment. "It's okay, Dan. I mean, we're just study partners," she said.

With those words, he cut his eyes toward Annie. He squinted, looking at her in disbelief. The look on his face was one she had not seen before. He didn't look mad. It was more of a hurtful look. He walked toward the door and paused before turning the handle. "Just study partners, huh? If only you knew," he whispered, as he walked out the door.

****

Annie tossed and turned all night. The last time she looked at the clock it read 3:25 a.m. *Good going. You really messed it up now.* She sobbed into her pillow, until she finally drifted to sleep.

With the morning light, came proof she had been crying. Her eyes were red and swollen. *How can I face him today?* After an hour of struggling with the desire to stay home, she knew the importance of attending Riley's class. Her grade depended on it.

After Annie pulled into the parking lot, she opened the mirror in her sun visor and inspected her face. It was still obvious she had been crying. She removed the compact from her purse and applied more concealer under her eyes. She was waiting for Kim to arrive, hoping she would have an opportunity to talk before class.

When Kim finally arrived, Annie noticed Darren was in the passenger's seat. She knew she wouldn't be able to talk with her now. Annie put on a fake smile as they walked toward her.

They were holding hands and laughing. Kim grasped Annie's arm. "You're not going to believe it, but Jill has agreed to go to church on Sunday. Isn't that great?"

Annie nodded. "Yeah, that's great."

Kim proceeded to tell Annie about the meeting with Jill, and how things were really turning around for teen.

Tears began flowing down Annie's cheeks, and it didn't take long for Kim to notice. "Oh, my Gosh! Annie, what's wrong?"

Embarrassed, Annie looked at Darren, then looked back at Kim. "It's nothing," she said, wiping away her tears.

Kim whispered something to Darren and he politely excused himself.

Annie pointed toward the bench in the courtyard. "Can we go over there?" she asked.

Kim followed Annie. "What is it?" Kim asked, as she pushed a strand of hair from Annie's face.

Annie bit the corner of her lip, as tears flowed down her cheeks. "I made such a fool of myself last night."

Kim took a tissue from her purse and handed it to Annie. "Why?" she asked.

Annie told Kim about how she hurt Dan and what he said when he left. "I don't know, Kim, he's so hard to figure out." She continued wiping the tears from the corner of her eyes. "You were right. I guess I like him more than I realized. Sometimes I think he likes me and then sometimes I think it couldn't be possible," Annie said.

Kim looked confused. "I don't understand, Annie. Why couldn't it be possible?" Kim asked.

Annie shrugged her shoulders. "I just can't see someone like him being interested in someone like me," Annie said.

Kim winked at Annie. "I think sometimes you underestimate yourself. "You're pretty, smart, and everyone likes you," Kim said.

Annie wiped her cheek. "Not anymore," Annie said.

Kim put her arm around Annie as they walked into the building. "Annie, I know you're scared and this is new to you, but maybe you should tell Dan how you feel. There's nothing wrong with having feelings for him," Kim said.

Annie was silent.

"Think about it, Annie. You really need to talk to him." Kim said.

Annie sighed. "Things used to be so easy before he came into the picture," Annie said.

Kim laughed. "It was bound to happen sooner or later, Annie."

"I'm just so embarrassed to face him again," Annie said.

Kim looked over Annie's shoulder and gave her a sympathetic look. "Don't look now, but he just walked into Riley's class."

Annie closed her eyes. "I don't think I can go in there," she said.

Kim nodded toward the classroom as the bell rang. "It will be okay. Just follow me," she said.

Annie walked toward the back of the classroom, avoiding all eye contact with Dan. Mr. Riley announced they would be watching a film, portraying various social classes in society. He explained this was a correlation to their current assignments. Annie was glad they watched a film, because this helped camouflage her discomfort. Although the room was dark, she could hear him breathing and felt his presence.

As the bell rang, Dan gathered his books and walked outside the classroom. He didn't say a word to Annie and she was somewhat relieved. She knew Kim was right and she needed to talk to him, but she was too ashamed. *Tell him the truth. Tell him you enjoy his company and have feelings for him.*

She gathered her books and walked to her car. It was hard to believe that just two weeks ago, Dan came into her life. For the first time ever, she felt excitement and frustration at the same time. She couldn't believe such a wonderful friendship was now ruined by words; words she would take back if she could. She loved spending time with Dan and wondered if he would call again. How would they handle the assignment?

Annie opened her car door and found a white envelope in her seat. She placed her purse on the passenger seat and opened the envelope. It was a letter. She glanced at the bottom of the letter and saw that it was from Dan. She scanned the parking lot to see if she could see his car, but he wasn't there. She trembled as she held the letter between her fingers.

Dear Annie,

It's almost midnight and I couldn't sleep after thinking about what happened tonight. Part of me wanted to call you, but I decided against it. I was too hurt. I thought about what you said. God knows I have replayed our conversation over and over in my mind.

First, I would like to address the girlfriend comment. After thinking about things from your perspective, I could see how you would be suspicious, but let me assure you that I don't have a girlfriend. I haven't even been on a date in eight months. The calls were from my parents and that is all I want to say about it right now. Please don't question me about it. In time, I will tell you. I know you may not understand this, but just know I'm being honest when I tell you, I would never lie to you, Annie.

I have to be honest and tell you I was hurt when you said we were "just study partners." I know I have no right to be upset, because we haven't known each other very long, but I thought we were a little more than "just study partners." I'm sorry if I misunderstood our relationship.

I have to tell you I was very excited to find out you were going to be my study partner, as you like

to call it. I was so nervous when we went to the lake and I just prayed I wouldn't say anything stupid. I have really enjoyed spending time with you and getting to know you. I didn't know if I made you feel uncomfortable when I held your hand and I wasn't sure what you meant when you asked if it was intentional. I did mean it. Looking back, I wish I had turned my phone off.

I have a confession to make. I saw what you wrote in your notebook that day in the courtyard. I pretended not to see it because it would have been too presumptuous on my part to think it was my name. I convinced myself it had to be another Dan, but I secretly hoped you were writing about me. Were you? I also heard you talking to Kim about Mark. I then knew I had jumped to conclusions.

Annie, we have to complete this assignment and I want to do whatever I can to make you feel comfortable. Okay, here goes the kicker. I care about you, probably more than I should. I think you know that. It's hard for me to hide my feelings with you. I'm pretty sure you know that too.

We have to find a way to work together and put this behind us. If you want to be just "study partners," I'm fine with this. If you want to be friends, then I'll be the best friend I can be to you. I'm going to leave this up to you.

It's much easier writing this, than telling you face to face, and who knows if I will even get the nerve up to give you this letter. I just know I have to get this off my chest.

I'm going to the lake after class. If you want to talk, well, you know where I'll be. You can also try me on my cell phone. I just realized I never gave you my number. I know I make you uncomfort-

**able at times and you're probably too scared to
come to the lake, but please try. I think we need
to talk.**
(706)777-9999.

Love,
Dan

Annie stared at the letter. She felt a sense of bittersweet
emotions. She was elated he cleared up any misconceptions
she had. She was even more relieved he admitted to having
feelings for her, but what would she do now? Annie knew
she had to admit her feelings, but she was ashamed about
the way she talked to him. How would she face him? How
would she tell him that he was all she could think about? This
wouldn't be easy for her. She had never cared for anyone
like this before and after all, it had only been two weeks.

Annie stared at the phone, trying to muster up the courage
to call him. She hesitated before dialing his number. As she
held the phone to her ear, she decided to end the call. "No!"
she whispered. This wasn't something that should be dealt
with over the phone. She knew she made a mistake and hurt
him badly. He deserved an apology – face to face.

As she drove to the lake, she visualized their conversation. She practiced what she would say, but nothing seemed
to sound right. How could she face him knowing he saw
what she had written in her notebook? Although he admitted
in the letter that he hoped it was his name, how could she tell
him? She knew she couldn't lie to him, but she felt anxious
about admitting it.

It took everything in her to continue driving, when part
of her wanted to turn around and go home. As she drove
through the gate, she saw his car from a distance. Her heart
pounded rapidly. She could see a figure sitting on top of

the picnic table by the water. He was facing the water and seemed oblivious to the parking lot behind him.

Annie got out of the car and began walking slowly toward him. When she swallowed, she could feel a lump developing in her throat. *It's not too late to turn around.* She paused for a moment, before approaching the table. She was at a loss for words, but knew she had to think of something.

When she came into his sight, he looked up, raised his eyebrows, and stared at her in amazement. Her heart pounded rapidly as they made eye contact. Just as he was about to speak, he refrained and smiled. Neither of them said anything for a few seconds, but his smile let her know he was glad she was there.

"I.... didn't think you would come," he confessed.

Not knowing what to say, Annie nodded, as she held the folded letter between her fingers. Dan glanced at the letter then into her eyes. He sighed before speaking. "Look, Annie. It was late when I wrote it and I...,"

Before he could finish, Annie interrupted. "No, Dan. I was wrong, so wrong for talking to you like that. I was wrong for, well, you know, jumping to conclusions when it was really none of my business," she confessed.

Dan shook his head. "No, you had every reason to get upset with me. I should have told you about the phone calls," he said.

Annie felt a lump in her throat again. "Dan, you have nothing to apologize for, really, it was all my fault," she confessed, as she moved closer to the table. She took a seat beside him and clasped her hands together. She had so much to say, but the words weren't forming. Kim was right; she owed it to him to admit her feelings.

As she took a deep breath, they began speaking at the same time. Dan flashed a smile that melted her heart. "You first," he said.

Annie rubbed the back of her neck, as she felt sweat beads forming. "Dan, I'm not good at this. The truth is I never had a serious boyfriend, and well, I." She paused, trying to find the courage to continue, but felt frozen.

"Annie," he whispered.

She glanced into his eyes, knowing she had to reveal the truth. She sighed again.

He wanted to reach for her hand, but didn't know how she felt about him. Was she about to tell him that she never had a serious boyfriend and wasn't ready for a relationship? He needed to hear the truth.....good or bad. "Annie, please talk to me," he said.

She slowly shook her head, as she studied the serious expression on his face. "This is so hard," she admitted.

Dan offered a sympathetic smile. "It doesn't have to be. Just be honest," he said.

Annie exhaled sharply. "You're right. You deserve to hear the truth," she said. They sat there in silence for a minute, before she felt comfortable. He shifted his eyes from her to the lake, hoping she would have an easier time talking if he wasn't staring at her.

"I, well you see. I have never cared for anyone before. Not like this," she admitted. "I like you, Dan. The truth is…I like you a lot, and I think that scared me."

Dan closed his eyes. She cared about him. He felt relieved to hear her say that. As he glanced toward her, he noticed she was nervously twirling her bracelet around her wrist. He reached for her hand. "Annie," he whispered.

She looked into his eyes. "I'm making a mess of this, aren't I?" she asked.

He smiled as he began tracing small circles on top of her hand. "You're doing just fine. Please tell me everything you want to say. I opened up to you in my letter and I want us to be completely honest with each other," he said.

Annie nodded and hesitated before continuing. "It's strange. I have really enjoyed our time together, but I was so scared I was reading too much into it. I didn't know how you felt, until this," she said, as she fanned the letter.

"Now you know," he said.

She nodded. "Yeah, now I know."

Dan leaned forward and cupped his hands together. "I'm relieved to hear you say that because I was genuinely hurt when you referred to us as "just study partners." He lowered his head and stared at the ground. "I felt a connection to you, and I thought you felt the same way until last night," he said.

Annie frowned. "I know, and for that I'm very sorry," she said.

Dan lifted his head and stared into her eyes. "Can I ask you a question?" he asked.

"Uh huh," she said.

"The name in your notebook…. Was it me?"

Annie closed her eyes, not wanting to answer the question. Why did he have to ask her?

"Annie," he whispered.

Feeling embarrassed, she nodded. "Yes, it was you," she whispered.

Dan reached for her hand, but this time he didn't let go. "Thank you," he whispered.

CHAPTER ELEVEN

Blissful thoughts of Dan and the weekend made it difficult for Annie to concentrate in her Political Science class. Dan promised to take her out for pizza that night and although, she wasn't looking forward to the ridiculous chores that Mrs. Hildebrand concocted; she was looking forward to spending time with Dan.

As she traced stick figures and flowers in her notebook, she was surprised when her cell phone beeped. Annie looked around the room, hoping that nobody heard the beep, especially her professor. Everyone seemed to be oblivious to the noise. Some of the students were taking notes, while others were engaged in their own activities. Annie looked at her phone and realized she had a text message. This was odd since Kim never sent text messages during class. Annie pressed the read text message button.

"Just thinking about you. Can't wait to see you tonight. I'm counting down the minutes." Love Dan.

Annie smiled, as she discretely typed a reply.

"Funny....I was just thinking about you too. 5:30 p.m.?"

She looked around the room once more to make sure that nobody noticed what she was doing. She wondered if Dan would respond again. Just as she was about to place her phone back into her purse, she heard another beep.

"Good to know you're thinking about me too. Yes, 5:30 p.m. I have a few errands to run, so I'll pick you up then. Looking forward to it."

Just as she was about to type another response, the bell rang. She gathered her books and purse and ran to her car.

****

Annie had an hour and fifteen minutes to get ready before Dan arrived. She placed hot rollers in her long, dark hair and reapplied blush and lip-gloss. The pizza parlor was a casual atmosphere, but she wanted to look her best. She slipped on a pair of jeans and a pink baby doll shirt. After trying on two pairs of shoes, she decided on the pink pumps she had purchased the summer before.

Knowing that it would take a while for the rollers to curl her hair, Annie decided to call Kim. She was anxious to tell her about the lake and how well things had turned out. She knew Kim would be proud and maybe even a little shocked. Annie glanced at the clock before dialing her number.

"Hey Kim. It's me," Annie chimed in.

"Well, it's about time. I have been worried sick about you since yesterday. Why didn't you call me last night?" Kim asked.

Annie sighed. "I know. I'm sorry, but after I got home last night it was so late and I had to finish a paper. I have so much to tell you."

"Well? Come on. I'm dying to know," Kim confessed.

"Okay, okay," Annie laughed. "After Riley's class, I found a note in my car from Dan. He explained everything and asked me to meet him at the lake."

"Geez, the lake again. Is that the only place he knows?" Kim joked.

Annie laughed. "He likes it there. Anyway, he doesn't have a girlfriend and he said that he hasn't been on a date in eight months. The calls were from his parents."

"But why wouldn't he answer? I don't understand why he would ignore his parents," Kim said.

Annie touched her hand to a roller to see if it had cooled. "Well, that part is still a mystery, but he asked me not to question him about it. He said he would tell me when the time was right. I have to believe him, especially after everything he said in the letter and what happened at the lake," Annie said.

"What happened?" Kim asked.

Annie took a deep breath. "He admitted to caring about me. He said that he's happy we're study...whoops, I'm not supposed to say that anymore."

"Not supposed to say what?" Kim asked.

"Study partners. He hates that. Anyway, he asked me about the name in my notebook."

"Really?" Kim laughed. "And ...did you tell him the truth?"

"Yes and then some. You'll be glad to know I confessed to having feelings for him too. I apologized profusely for hurting him and told him I was just scared," Annie said.

"Good girl. I'm so proud of you Annie. I know how difficult it must have been, but I'm glad you told him. Listen, I know I have been somewhat pushy about you finding someone, but I wanted you to be happy. It worried me that you wouldn't let anyone get close to you. It's not healthy," Kim explained.

"I know and I love you for that," Annie said.

"I love you too."

Annie glanced at the clock. "Well, I better finish getting ready. Dan will be here in thirty minutes."

"Oh, Annie before you go, I wanted to tell you that Jill will be coming to church on Sunday. Darren will be there too. Isn't that great?" Kim asked.

"Good. I'm looking forward to meeting her." Annie was happy that Jill had agreed to come to church.

"Annie, I just thought of something. Why don't you invite Dan?" Kim asked.

Annie hesitated. "I don't know. I mean I thought about it, but I don't know how to ask. He brought it up one time, but I don't know if he would come," Annie said.

"Well, think about it and I'll talk to you sometime tomorrow," Kim said.

Annie stared at herself in the mirror and decided if the subject came up, she would mention it to him.

Dan was prompt as usual. Annie peeked through the curtains in her room and watched him as he got out of the car. He was wearing jeans and a dark blue polo shirt. *You are so gorgeous*, she thought.

His eyes widened as she opened the door. "Wow, you look really...." he paused, unable to say another word.

"Really what?" she laughed.

He smiled. "Breath taking," he admitted. He couldn't believe how different she looked with her hair curled.

Annie smiled, as she studied his expression. "So do you," she said.

They seemed to be more at ease with each other and their conversation lacked the intimidation they had previously struggled with. The pizza parlor was crowded, but they didn't mind waiting fifteen minutes before being seated. They were so engaged in conversation that the minutes flew by quickly.

"How much do you think we'll get done tomorrow?" Annie asked, as she took a bite out of the pizza.

Dan laughed. "Well, by the looks of that list, I think we'll be lucky to complete two jobs," he said.

Annie pushed her glass to the edge of the table, as the server poured more tea. "Where do we begin?" she asked.

Dan raised his eyebrows and grinned. "Oh, I'm sure she'll let us know."

After they finished their meal, they held hands as they walked to the car. He opened her car door and waited until she was situated before closing the door. She smiled as he slowly glanced away, backing out of the parking space.

The warm air filled the car, as Dan rolled down his window. "Will this bother you?" he asked.

"No, it's such a beautiful night," Annie said.

Dan reached for Annie's hand and it was evident that neither of them wanted to let go. When they arrived at her house, Dan opened the car door for Annie, as he always did. He held her hand until they reached the front door. "How does nine o'clock sound?" he asked.

Annie raised her eyebrows. "Isn't that kind of early for a late riser?" she teased. He smirked. "You're funny. I never said that I couldn't get up early. I prefer not to get up early on a Saturday. Anyway, Mrs. H. might chastise us if we're too late getting started."

Annie nodded. "You're right about that."

Dan smiled, as he watched her nervously search her purse for her house key. She glanced up, noticing he had a sheepish grin.

"What's so funny?" she asked.

He nodded toward the front door that was already open. The sound of the television could be heard through the screen door.

She playfully slapped his arm. "That's real funny," she said. "You allowed me to panic for no reason."

His smile slowly faded into a serious expression, as he carefully contemplated kissing her. "I really had a great time tonight," he said.

She twirled the key ring around her finger. "Me too," she said, as she nervously acknowledged her intuition. *Is he going to kiss me?* She timidly backed away, allowing more room between them.

He sensed her discomfort and kissed her gently on the cheek.

Annie admired him for being such a gentleman. She was glad he didn't rush things and treated her like a lady. This eased her insecurities about being in a relationship. She chuckled, as she realized she was actually in a relationship now.

He held her hands in front of him, as he gave them a gentle squeeze. "I better be going now," he said. "I'll be here at nine," he reiterated.

Annie watched him as he walked to his car. "Bye," she called out.

"Sweet dreams," he said.

CHAPTER TWELVE

Annie was waiting on the front porch when Dan arrived. "Nine o'clock on the dot," she called out.

Dan smiled. "Well, we wouldn't want to keep Mrs. Hildebrand waiting, now would we?" he said, in a playful, sarcastic tone.

Annie laughed. "I know, I actually dreamed about her last night."

"Oh, and here I thought you dreamed about me," he said.

Annie laughed, as he opened the car door for her. Little did he know how much of that statement was really true. Dan was all she had thought about for the last two weeks.

Mrs. Hildebrand was working in her flowerbeds when they arrived. She made no attempt to engage in small talk, as she motioned for them to follow her. As they followed her into what appeared to be an old, but well preserved shed, she showed them where all of the tools and supplies were kept. "George always kept his building immaculate and this is how I like to keep it as well," she said.

"George was your husband?" Annie asked.

Mrs. Hildebrand nodded. "Yes, that's right."

Dan focused his attention to a workbench that displayed several glass figurines. They were in every shape and color. "What a magnificent pair of doves," Dan said.

Watching him carefully, Mrs. Hildebrand walked to the bench and picked up the glass figure. "Yes, I remember when George did this one," she said. Her face transformed into a serene expression. "He was a glassmaker, you know, very talented and articulate. He made this one the year before he died," she explained.

Annie and Dan looked in amazement, as she explained the stories behind every figurine. Talking about her husband seemed to soften her mood. She was less harsh than their previous meetings.

"Well, we better get started," Dan said.

Mrs. Hildebrand pointed to the paint and brushes. "I was really hoping you could fix my bird feeder today. The poor little things don't have any place to eat," she said.

It was a strange turn of events, because Mrs. Hildebrand's demeanor had changed. She wasn't spouting orders like they had envisioned. She was actually very pleasant. Annie wondered if this was attributed to the old lady being happy about getting her chores done free.

"Yes, ma'am, I'll fix the bird feeder before I do anything else," Dan said.

Mrs. Hildebrand turned to Annie. "I was thinking you could help me plant the impatiens."

Annie smiled. "I don't have a green thumb, but if you show me what you want done, I'll be glad to do it," she said.

"Have you planted flowers before?" Mrs. Hildebrand asked.

Annie shook her head. "I used to help my mom, but I don't know if I remember how," she confessed.

Mrs. Hildebrand nodded. "You never forget. Practice is all you need, but you never forget."

Dan remained in the building and the pounding of a hammer echoed from within. It was obvious he was repairing the birdfeeder.

Annie was pleasantly surprised by his positive attitude. She knelt beside Mrs. Hildebrand, as they planted nine rows of impatiens in a semi-circular pattern. The violet flowers were the most vibrant.

Mrs. Hildebrand asked Annie to finish the last row while she attended to some business in the house. The elderly lady walked away slowly, as she made her way toward the side entrance.

The sun was hot and Annie felt the heat on the back of her neck. She glanced toward the building. Dan wiped his forehead as he dabbed some white paint on the faded birdfeeder.

"Looks good," she called out.

"Thanks. I think it's finally revived. The flowers look good too," he said.

Annie finished planting the last flower when Mrs. Hildebrand opened the side door. "Please come inside," she ordered.

Dan and Annie looked at each other with curiosity. As they walked toward the house, Dan joked that she was probably going to scold them.

"Come in, come in quickly before the flies get in," she said. Dan smiled at Annie. This was one of the sayings he mocked. They followed her into the kitchen where she had prepared their lunch. They looked at each other, not sure if their eyes were deceiving them.

"Mrs. Hildebrand, you didn't have to do this," Annie said.

Mrs. Hildebrand waved her hand. "Nonsense. You have to eat, and besides, you are helping me. You can wash up in there," she said, as she pointed to the powder room.

Mrs. Hildebrand prepared chicken salad with grapes and pecans, a large bowl of fresh fruit, and a tray of various cheeses and crackers. She poured two large glasses of peach iced tea. For dessert, she served vanilla ice cream with lemon tarts. Mrs. Hildebrand joined them as they savored every bite of their lunch.

"This is the best chicken salad I have ever eaten," Annie remarked.

Mrs. Hildebrand smiled. "Mamma's good ol' recipe."

Annie helped Mrs. Hildebrand clear the table, while Dan excused himself and returned to the building. Annie watched Dan through the window as she stacked the dishes on the counter.

"Is he courting you?" Mrs. Hildebrand asked.

Annie turned around in amazement, not knowing what to say. "Pardon me?"

"Is he courting you?" Mrs. Hildebrand repeated.

Annie could feel her cheeks turn hot. "I.... I'm not quite sure what you mean, Mrs. Hildebrand."

The elderly lady continued placing containers in the refrigerator, not realizing she had embarrassed Annie. "Oh, dear. I keep forgetting that you young people don't refer to it as courting anymore."

Annie looked perplexed. It wasn't the term that confused her. She was confused because she wasn't sure if she and Dan were "courting." After all, they just ironed out their problems. How would she answer the question, though? Annie smiled. "Dan and I are in the same class and our professor assigned us as partners for this assignment. That's how we met," Annie explained.

Mrs. Hildebrand raised her eyebrows. "I see," she said softly.

Dan knocked on the screen door. "Mrs. H. Can you please come out here and see what you think?" he asked.

"Mrs. H.?" Annie whispered.

Dan winked.

Mrs. Hildebrand cupped her cheeks. "Oh, my goodness. Would you look at that? It looks better than it did when we bought it," she exclaimed.

Dan smiled at her approval. "I secured it with extra nails so it should hold up nicely. I'll hang it for you after the paint has dried," he said.

Mrs. Hildebrand clasped her hands together and smiled. "That would be lovely."

"Well, what would you like done now?" Dan asked.

The elderly lady shook her head. "That's enough for one day. Why don't you come inside and you can ask me some more questions for your little project."

Dan pulled at his shirt, examining the paint and grime that covered the white fabric. "We're going to do this now?" he whispered to Annie.

Annie grinned, as she shrugged her shoulders. They were both sunburned and exhausted from the heat, not to mention they needed showers.

"Well, do you mind if we come back tomorrow night or Monday? I could really use a shower before we sit down and talk," Dan said.

Mrs. Hildebrand glanced at the clock. "Why don't you go home and get yourselves cleaned up and come back tonight? It's the weekend, so you don't have to retire early," she said.

Annie found her expressions to be amusing. "Retire, partake, courting."

Dan and Annie agreed. "Well, if you're sure we wouldn't be intruding, I guess we'll see you later," Dan said.

Annie dosed off during the short ride back to her house. Dan thought she looked like an angel with her head turned toward him, and resting comfortably on the headrest. When they arrived at her house, he walked her to the front door and they agreed he would pick her up at six o'clock. That would give them an hour and thirty minutes to get cleaned up. Annie was glad he suggested this, because she didn't like feeling dirty and sweaty around him.

****

Annie jerked away from the water as it glided down her sunburned neck. The pain was excruciating. She could barely stand to brush the back of her hair. Annie slipped on a pink floral sundress and let her hair fall down her back. She was anxious to return to Mrs. Hildebrand's house so they could complete the second assessment.

Annie decided to wait inside since the air was still muggy. She knew Dan would be on time, but she couldn't bear the thought of being in the heat. Annie was watching television when Dan knocked on the door. He surprised her with flowers when she opened the screen door.

"Oh, how sweet of you," she said, with a smile.

"I am, aren't I?" he said.

He followed her into the kitchen while she searched the cupboards for a vase.

"Wow, your face really got a lot of sun," she said.

"Yeah, I know. Shaving was a real blast."

Annie laughed. I know. My neck feels like someone took a blow torch to it."

They agreed it had been a good day, despite being sunburned. Mrs. Hildebrand was more than cordial; she was pleasant.

Mrs. Hildebrand was peering through the window when they pulled into her driveway. She greeted them as if they were long-lost friends. They followed her into the parlor where, she poured two glasses of her famous peach iced tea.

She smiled as she watched them sip the tea. She remembered how much they bragged about the flavor during lunch. "I phoned my sister in West Virginia and told her you restored my bird feeder and she couldn't believe it."

Dan smiled. "Well, I'm just glad you're happy with it."

"Yes and thanks to Annie, my flower beds are now completed." Mrs. Hildebrand covered her mouth as she snickered. "I always send Nellie, my sister I was telling you about, pictures of my flowers. I like to rub it in since she couldn't grow a weed if she tried."

Dan and Annie laughed as Mrs. Hildebrand bragged about her impatiens and how her sister accused her of being pompous. It was evident that Mrs. Hildebrand found the charade comical.

Dan smiled as he opened the packet and patiently waited for her to finish her stories. As he glanced at the second assessment, Mrs. Hildebrand cupped her cheek in her hand.

"Oh, listen to me go on and on about nonsense. You're not here to listen to an old woman's boring stories."

Annie offered a sincere smile. "Oh, on the contrary. We're enjoying this very much. It makes the assignment more personal," she said.

Mrs. Hildebrand placed her hand on her chest and smiled. "That's very kind of you, but we need to stay on schedule. I'm sure you're eager to ask your questions and leave."

It was true they were eager to ask the questions and learn more about her, but they were in no hurry to leave.

Dan clicked his pen open and flipped through the pages until he found the questions. "Mrs. Hildebrand, can you tell us why the best time of your life was when you were in your thirties?"

She gazed at the portrait of her beloved husband, as she began to speak. "George and I were well-established when that picture was taken. It wasn't always that way, though. We packed up everything we owned, which wasn't much, and left West Virginia," she said.

"You came here?" Annie asked.

Mrs. Hildebrand nodded. "Yes, we moved to Georgia because George's father owned a glass factory. We struggled the first five years of our marriage, while George tried desperately to find work in West Virginia. He knew I wanted to stay near my family, but there was no work there.... except the mines. I knew George wouldn't be content working the mines," she explained.

Dan and Annie were sitting on the edge of the sofa, holding on to every word the woman muttered. She was no longer providing one-word answers. They weren't sure what happened to change her mind, but they were glad she was being more accommodating.

"George must have loved you very much to have stayed in West Virginia so long," Annie remarked.

Mrs. Hildebrand nodded. "He did, indeed. We literally transformed from rags to riches when he went to work for his father. Little did we know that ten years later, George would take over the factory."

"His father passed?" Dan asked.

"No, his father suffered from arthritis and his hands became too weak and decrepit to work in the factory. George was an overnight success. He soon purchased this house among many other things. I attribute everything we ever had to George's hard work and determination," she explained.

Annie looked around the room at the exquisite paintings. "Well, you have a beautiful home, Mrs. Hildebrand." Annie was dying to ask about the ring, but she feared this would appear rude and cause Mrs. Hildebrand to revert to her previous demeanor. She couldn't take that chance. Her grade... their grade, depended on this.

Dan and Annie were pleased this conversation had more substance, than the prior one. They wouldn't have to fabricate any of the details for this assessment.

Annie scooted to the edge of the couch and leaned forward. "How did you and George meet?"

Mrs. Hildebrand smiled, as her eyes sparkled with intensity. "It was love at first sight. Harry, my oldest brother, came home from the war. I still remember that day. Mamma,

Daddy and I went to pick him up at the port, but there beside him... was the best- looking sailor I had ever seen. I couldn't take my eyes off him. He was tall and had broad shoulders. George was passing through on his way home to Georgia and, of course, Mamma and Daddy were more than happy to accommodate one of Harry's friends. He only stayed three days, but it was the best three days of my life. It's amazing how quickly you come to know someone," she explained.

Dan and Annie glanced at each other, realizing the similarity of their relationship. "So he stayed in West Virginia?" Annie asked.

Mrs. Hildebrand sighed. "No, he went to Georgia, but we wrote to each other every day. We did this for two months," she said.

"He came back?" Dan asked.

"He came back," Mrs. Hildebrand whispered. "We wed shortly after that."

"Did you have any children?" Annie asked.

Mrs. Hildebrand stared out the window. "No, we weren't able to have children. They didn't have all of the medical advancements they have nowadays," she responded.

It was almost eight o'clock and although Mrs. Hildebrand was being very accommodating, they took their cue when she glanced at the clock.

"Well, Mrs. Hildebrand, we really enjoyed this time with you and we appreciate you being candid and open about your life," Dan said.

Annie clasped her hands together and shrugged. "When can we come back and talk with you some more?" she asked.

Mrs. Hildebrand said they could return on Tuesday.

Dan and Annie were elated to have gathered so much information. As they walked to the car, Annie turned around to see if Mrs. Hildebrand was watching them. She caught a glimpse of the elderly lady's face as she slowly disappeared behind a curtain.

"Are you okay?" Dan asked.

Annie nodded. "Yeah, let's go."

The short drive back to Annie's house was quiet. As Dan pulled into the driveway, Annie felt a sense of sadness. She didn't want the night to end...not yet. It dawned on her that she had forgotten to ask Dan about church. How would she bring this up?

"Where's your father's truck?" Dan asked.

Annie suddenly remembered that after much persuasion, he agreed to go bowling with two of his friends from the hardware store. She had to beg him to go. Her father felt guilty if he participated in anything fun. Annie told him in a loving way that her mother would have wanted him to enjoy life.

Dan followed Annie to the porch swing. The air was cool, with the hint of a breeze. As the swing began to sway, Dan moved closer to Annie. As she curled her hands under the wooden planks of the swing, she inhaled deeply as she breathed in the fresh air.

He patted her hand. "Are we okay now?" he asked.

Annie glanced into his eyes. She loved the way his blue eyes sparkled in the moonlight. She tucked the corner of her lip in. "Yeah, we're good," she said.

He reached for Annie's hand. "Is this okay?"

Without saying a word, she nodded as she continued looking into his eyes. After a few seconds, she managed to muster up the courage to bring up the topic of church. "Are you going to come over tomorrow?" she asked.

Dan playfully leaned his shoulder into Annie's. "Do you want me to?"

Annie smiled. "Do you really have to ask that question?" She could feel Dan staring at her.

"Well?" he asked.

She shrugged. "Well what?"

"I'm waiting for an answer."

Embarrassed, Annie turned her head away and remained silent.

"Okay, you don't have to answer that," he said.

Annie turned toward him. "Yes. The answer is yes. I want you to come over tomorrow," she said.

Not wanting to embarrass her again, he maintained a serious tone. "What time?" he asked.

This was her chance she thought. "Ten thirty would be good. This should give us plenty of time to get to the church," she laughed.

"Okay," he said.

She glanced at him, wondering if he was being sincere. "Yeah, I'm sure you'll be here at ten thirty," she joked.

"I will."

Annie tilted her head and looked into his eyes. "Seriously?" she asked.

"Yes, seriously, unless you don't want me to go," he said.

Annie looked surprised. "Yes, most definitely, but..... I was afraid to ask," she confessed.

He gently squeezed her hand. "I was afraid you wouldn't ask."

Annie felt a rush of excitement run through her, as she sat on the swing, holding his hand. She found it difficult to comprehend that he was as taken with her as she was with him.

Dan gave her hand another gentle squeeze. "I should go now," he said.

She didn't want him to leave, but she was thankful to have spent the entire day with him. She nodded. As they stood, facing each other, Dan pulled her close. He didn't want to overstep his bounds, so he leaned down and kissed her on the cheek.

"Sweet dreams," he whispered, as his fingers gently released his grip.

"Bye," she whispered.

CHAPTER THIRTEEN

Annie paced back in forth in her room, while she waited for the hot rollers to curl her hair. She couldn't understand why she was so nervous. After all, she had hoped for this.

As she brushed through her hair, she convinced herself it was going to be a special day. Dan would accompany her to church and she would get to meet Jill. After church, Annie and Dan would work on the assessment and prepare for Tuesday evening. Annie had so much to tell Kim, but she knew that she wouldn't have an opportunity.

Annie understood that Kim was equally busy with Darren and their assignment, but she felt like their friendship was fading. Annie hoped that would never happen. She tried to convince herself that unusual circumstances were preventing them from spending so much time together. Once the eight weeks were up, they would have more time together.

Annie bit the corner of her lip. She never considered what would happen once the assignment had been completed. She hoped that her relationship with Dan would continue.

"Annie," her father called, "Dan's here."

Annie checked herself in the mirror one more time and grabbed her purse.

"You look beautiful," he said as his eyes scanned the eloquent, but conservative black dress she was wearing.

Annie glanced across the room at her father, who was reading the paper. She was elated to hear that he thought she was beautiful, but she hoped her father wasn't listening. She didn't need that embarrassment. "I was just about to say the same thing," Annie said.

Dan was wearing black pinstriped pants and a crisp, white, ironed shirt with a striking red and black tie. Although he always looked handsome, there was something about his church attire that made him even more attractive.

"We're leaving, Daddy," she yelled. "You're welcome to go with us."

Her father smiled as he peeked over the paper. "Maybe next time," he said.

"He always says that," Annie whispered to Dan, as they walked out the door.

****

Dan and Annie caught a glimpse of Kim, Darren and Jill as they were walking into the church. "There she is," Annie pointed. "That's Jill."

Dan reached behind him and retrieved his Bible from the back seat.

Annie looked stunned. "You have a Bible?" she asked.

Dan wrinkled his forehead. "Yeah, doesn't everybody?"

Annie felt bad for assuming he didn't own a Bible. She led the way as they slipped into the pew beside Kim and Darren.

"Wow, what a nice surprise," Kim said, as she waved to Dan. "You know Darren from class, and this is Jill," she said.

Darren smiled as he nodded, but Jill didn't offer a handshake. She looked terrified and Annie wasn't quite sure what to say.

"Nice to meet you, Jill," Annie said.

Jill slightly curled her lips, but said nothing.

"She's a little shy," Kim whispered.

Annie sat beside Kim. "I have so much to tell you," she said.

Kim nodded. "I know, me too."

"I miss you," Annie said.

"Me too. We have to make time for lunch next Wednesday," Kim said.

Annie smiled, knowing that Kim felt the same way. They decided not to join the rest of the choir since they had visitors. Everyone was instructed to stand and sing the last song. She felt spiritual as they sang her favorite song, "Blessed Assurance."

Annie stopped singing at the sound of Dan's voice. It was audible enough for her to determine that he had a beautiful voice. She was surprised that he didn't open the songbook, yet knew every word.

The preacher talked about God's love and how everyone is his child. He went on to explain that God loves his children no matter what they do.

Annie observed Jill during the invitation song. She prayed that God would give the troubled girl the peace she needed. Kim gave Annie a subtle nod, signifying their coincidental thoughts. Jill remained motionless as they stood for the last verse. Her knuckles were white from firmly gripping the pew.

The preacher held up his hand, indicating the conclusion of the invitation, then finished with the closing prayer. Kim's forehead creased as she picked up her Bible and followed behind Darren and Jill. "I was really hoping….," Kim whispered.

Annie patted Kim on the back. "Just give her some time. This is all new to her."

They walked to their cars and talked for a few minutes before going their separate ways.

After Annie and Dan got into the car, she glanced toward him, as he loosened his tie. "You're full of surprises today," she said.

"What do you mean?" he asked.

"What I mean is that you have been holding out on me."

"Holding out? I don't"....

"You have a beautiful voice," she interrupted. I couldn't hear you very well, but what I heard was inspiring," she said.

Dan grinned. "Thanks, but I think you need a hearing aid," he joked.

"I'm serious," she responded.

He smiled. "Hey I have an idea. Let's go back to the lake today," he suggested.

Annie laughed. "Ahhh, the lake. You're so predictable."

He winked. "Yeah, well, there's nothing wrong with being predictable."

"Okay, but can I ask you a question?" she asked.

"Sure," he replied.

"Why do you like going there so much?"

He smirked as he glanced between her and the road. "I have my reasons," he said.

As they pulled into her driveway, Dan reached for her hand. "Wait," he said. "I need to run home and take care of something and then I'll be back to pick you up."

Annie looked surprised. He never mentioned his home. She was dying to ask him if she could go along, but she knew he wouldn't allow that. She also knew that mentioning it would spark another argument. "Okay," she sighed.

Dan raised her hand to his lips. "It shouldn't take more than an hour. I just have to do something for my Mom, then I'll change clothes and pick you up."

This was the first time he mentioned his Mom and Annie wondered if he would start talking about his family. The only personal thing he had disclosed was that he had an older sister. He never mentioned her name though.

Annie's father was fixing a sandwich when she walked into the kitchen. "Where's Dan?" he asked.

Annie arranged two pieces of bread on her plate. "He had to go home and take care of something. He'll be back, though," she said.

Annie's father continued spreading mustard on his bread. "What are his folks like?" he asked.

Annie didn't quite know how to answer this. She didn't want to lie, but she knew he would find it odd that she had never met them. She placed a piece of ham on the bread. "I haven't actually met them yet. I think they stay pretty busy," she explained. Annie immediately changed the subject. "How was bowling?"

Her father laughed as he handed her the knife. "Let's just say I'm a little out of practice."

She sat at the table, watching her father chew slowly, as he perused the Sunday paper.

She was glad he didn't press her for more details about why she never met Dan's parents.

After she loaded her plate into the dishwasher, she kissed her father on the cheek. I'm going to change clothes then wait on the porch for Dan. I'll be back later," she said.

He glanced over the paper. "Okay, Honey. Be careful."

Annie flipped through the pages of a magazine, while she waited for Dan. She glanced between her watch and the street to see if she could see his car. It was now almost two o'clock. "Come on, Dan," she whispered.

As she tossed the magazine aside and walked to the edge of the porch, she considered calling his cell phone, but decided he would think she was too anxious. It was driving her crazy wondering what he was doing. She checked her cell phone to make sure she didn't miss his call.

Annie watched anxiously as a car turned down her street. She sighed as a sedan passed by her house. She sat back down in the swing and thumbed through the magazine again. After half an hour of nervously flipping through pages and pretending to read the contents of the magazine, she heard the sound of his engine approaching her street.

When he got out of the car and walked toward her, she could tell something was wrong. His face was red and he had a serious expression.

Annie rubbed his arm. "Everything okay?" she asked.

He nodded. "Yeah, ready to go?"

Annie stared at him while he buckled the seat belt, but he didn't seem to notice. She couldn't help but notice the forceful way he was shifting gears. He usually handled the car with such ease. She wanted to ask him again if everything was okay, but she knew the answer and feared how he would respond. With the radio turned off, the silence was more prevalent. She pretended to be oblivious to his demeanor, as she looked out the window.

When he pulled into the parking lot, he reached for her hand. As he glanced into her eyes, she saw the same pain she had seen the night she told him they were just study partners. He rested his head against the headrest, as he looked straight ahead. "I'm sorry," he whispered.

It was almost too much for her to look into his eyes. She felt helpless. "You have nothing to be sorry about," she said.

As they walked to their usual spot at the edge of the lake, Dan put his arm around her. It was obvious he was trying not to distance himself from her, despite his mood. They spread a blanket across the grass and sat side by side with their legs extended. Annie wondered if he sat beside her to avoid eye contact. Dan continued staring at the boats.

The silence was too much for Annie. "Jill seemed nice," she blurted out.

"Mmmmhmmm," he replied.

Annie sighed at his lack of emotion. "I'm really glad you went with me today," she said.

He reached for her hand. "Yeah, me too."

Although she refrained from showing frustration, she wanted to scream at him to talk to her. *Why can't you open up and talk to me? What is so bad in your life that you feel the need to shut me out?* These were questions she wanted to ask him.

Annie glanced at him then back at the ripples in the water. She tried desperately to think of something consoling to say. "You know you can talk to me," she said.

He nodded. "I know."

She wondered if he really believed her. "Dan, I don't know what happened after you left my house, but I really wish that you'd open up to me," she paused. "I feel like you know everything about me, but I don't know anything about you."

Dan lowered his head and squeezed her hand. She glanced his way, hoping he was about to disclose what was bothering him. Instead, he remained silent.

Annie took a deep breath, as she cupped her hands around his. "Look, I know you said in the letter you didn't want me to ask you anything about your parents, but you also said you cared about me." She bit the corner of her lip, hoping she wasn't making the situation worse.

He squinted, studying the concerned look on her face. "I do care about you," he said.

Their eyes locked for a moment then she looked away. "If that's true, why won't you tell me what's going on?" she asked.

Dan closed his eyes and shook his head. "Annie, please don't. I can't do this. Not right now," he said.

Annie sighed. "Why? What is so bad that you can't tell me?" she said.

Dan turned his head away from her. It was obvious he wasn't going to tell her.

Annie released her grip. "Fine. You don't have to tell me. I thought we were....." She looked away without saying another word.

Dan inched closer to her, as he put his arm around her shoulder. When he turned to look at her, their eyes locked again. "Soon," he whispered.

With her arms crossed, she raised her eyebrows.

He nodded. "I promise I'll tell you, but I just need some time. You have to trust me on this. I just need to figure some things out and I'll tell you everything," he continued.

Annie studied his expression, wondering if he really would tell her. She continued looking into his eyes. "Promise?" she asked.

"Yes, I promise," he said.

CHAPTER FOURTEEN

Dan and Annie spent two hours Monday afternoon in the library. Mr. Riley would be collecting the first synopsis on Tuesday. They took good notes, but it was going to be difficult to embellish on the first meeting with Mrs. Hildebrand. Once they completed the first portion, the remainder would be a breeze. Annie spoke aloud as she scribbled the words onto paper. Dan rested his hand on his cheek while he stared at her. He thought she looked so cute the way she looked up from the paper to seek his approval before continuing. He nodded as he offered her a warm smile.

Annie caught him staring a few times, but he pretended to look at the paper. He wondered how she would react if he told her the truth about his home life. She was so delicate and caring. It might be too much for her to handle.

"What do you think?" she asked.

Dan was startled. "Huh?" he asked.

"Earth to Dan," she said. "You seemed to be deep in thought."

He smiled. "Sorry, I was just thinking about how different Mrs. H. was on Saturday," he said.

Annie nodded. "Yeah, that was kind of strange. So how many carats do you think?"

"Carats?" he asked.

Annie giggled. "The ring, silly. How many carats do you think her ring is?"

Dan laughed. "You're just fascinated with that ring, aren't you?"

"Yes, aren't you curious about it?" she asked.

He smiled. "I'm curious why you're so fascinated with it," he said.

Annie shrugged and laughed. "I'm a girl. Girls love diamonds."

"Ahh, I see," he said, with a wink.

Annie playfully slapped his arm. "You're making fun of me."

He ran his finger down her nose. "Okay, I'll stop," he said.

Dan glanced at the clock on the wall. It was almost four o'clock. They agreed that the synopsis was as fine-tuned to perfection as they could get. As they walked to the parking lot, Dan hoped that Annie would ask him to come over. He didn't feel like going home so early. It was easier for him to get home late and avoid any interaction with his parents.

"Do you want to grab something to eat?" he asked.

Although it was difficult to decline his invitation, she knew she had to study for a Calculus test. As they reached her car, she tossed her books into the back seat.

Feeling disappointed, he faked a smile. "I'm going to miss you tonight," he said.

"Me too," she said. "I wish I didn't have to study for this test."

Dan nodded. "I know, I have a lot of homework too." He gently elbowed her. "I guess it won't kill me to be away from you one night."

She raised her eyebrows. "Are you sure you'll miss me?" she asked.

He smiled as he pressed his index finger against his thumb. "A little, I guess."

She pretended to pout. "Just a little?"

He winked. "You know better than that."

Annie secured her seat belt as Dan gently closed her door. She waited for him to get into his car before backing out. She watched him in the rear view mirror and waved as they turned in opposite directions.

Later that night, Annie spread her books across her bed, as she prepared to study for her test.

As she flipped through her notebook for a blank page, she found the page where she had scribbled their names. She smiled, wishing that he could be there with her, but she knew the importance of passing the Calculus test. She looked at her cell phone, hoping that if she stared long enough, he would call.

After studying for two hours, she closed her books and decided to get ready for bed. She took her cell phone into the bathroom while she brushed her teeth, in case he tried to call. After climbing into bed, she resigned to the fact that he probably wouldn't call her so she grabbed the book from her nightstand and flipped to the page she had marked the previous night.

****

The next day, Annie was surprised when she walked into Mr. Riley's class and Dan wasn't there. She couldn't imagine why he hadn't arrived yet. Dan was punctual for everything.

"Where's Dan?" Kim mouthed from across the classroom.

Annie shrugged her shoulders. She frantically watched the clock, hoping he would walk in at any moment, but it was too late. Mr. Riley closed the door as the bell rang. Annie reached into her purse to retrieve her cell phone. She wondered if Dan had left her a message. Just as she was about to send him a text message, he rushed in. Dan whispered something to Mr. Riley before approaching the back of the classroom.

Annie watched in anticipation. "Where were you?" she asked.

He had sweat beads dripping from his forehead. "The social worker left a message on my phone, saying Mrs. Hildebrand was hurt. Apparently, she took a pretty nasty fall, but thankfully, she didn't break anything," he whispered.

Annie's eyes widened. "Where is she?"

He leaned close to her ear. "She's still in the hospital. That's all of the information I have. I tried to call the hospital, but they put me on hold and I couldn't wait any longer," he explained.

Annie bit the corner of her lip. "What are we going to do?" she asked frantically.

"I don't know. We'll figure it out after class," he whispered.

Mr. Riley's voice could be heard, but Annie couldn't concentrate on what he was saying. She was hoping they would go to the hospital after class. Her heart ached for the elderly woman who had nobody. Annie's mind wandered back to their first meeting. Maybe Mrs. Hildebrand was cold toward them because she was lonely and miserable. Perhaps, she secretly enjoyed them being around and fabricated the list of chores as an excuse to prolong their visits. Whatever the reason, Annie knew they had to help.

After class, Annie and Dan made a dash to his car. As they pulled out of the parking lot, Dan handed his phone to Annie. "Hit redial," he said.

Annie pointed left, not knowing if Dan knew the location of the hospital. She held the phone to her ear. "Admissions please.... Hildebrand." Annie rolled her eyes. "Okay, thank you," she said.

Dan glanced between her and the road. "What did they say?" he asked.

Annie sighed. "They said she has been admitted, but couldn't provide information to anyone except family. It's so frustrating," she explained.

Dan cleared his throat. "We'll just see about that," he said.

As they walked toward the nurses' station, Annie peeked in every open door, hoping to find Mrs. Hildebrand. "Yes, we're here to see Mrs. Hildebrand," Dan said.

"Room 303," the nurse said, as she held two medicine trays in her hands.

Annie felt nervous as they read the numbers on every door. "Do you think she'll be mad that we came?" she asked.

Dan flashed a concerned look. "I don't know," he whispered.

When they arrived at her room, the door was partially closed. Annie's heart began to pound as Dan quietly pushed the door open. As they peeked around the curtain, Annie's eyes filled with tears at the sight of the frail woman. Mrs. Hildebrand was sleeping, despite the noise from all of the machines. Annie turned to look at Dan. He placed his hand on her back and guided her toward the bed. They stood by Mrs. Hildebrand's bedside, watching her chest rise with every breath. A tear rolled down Annie's cheek as she watched the liquid from the I.V. drip down the long plastic tube.

Mrs. Hildebrand slowly turned her head and her lips formed a partial smile. Her thin, white hair fanned across the pillow.

Annie struggled to fight back the tears as she reached for the lady's hand. "You scared us."

Mrs. Hildebrand patted Annie's hand. "No, no. Nothing to concern yourself with," she whispered.

Dan moved in closer. "Are you in pain?" he asked.

The elderly lady rubbed her shoulder. "A little tender here," she said.

"What happened?" Annie asked.

Mrs. Hildebrand squeezed Annie's hand. "Just a careless mistake. I was sweeping my front steps and lost my balance. The next thing I knew, Gertie came running across the street to help me."

Annie stroked the elderly lady's hair. "Thank God Gertie was outside," Annie said.

Mrs. Hildebrand nodded. "Mamma always said that if you take care of your neighbors, they will take care of you."

Dan flashed a sincere smile. "Well, we're just glad you're okay. "Did they say when you could go home?" he asked.

Mrs. Hildebrand squinted. "Let me think. I'm pretty sure they said Saturday... or was it Sunday?"

Annie shot Dan a concerned look. She wondered if the confusion was connected to the fall. "We'll verify it." Annie said. "Is there anything we can do for you?"

Mrs. Hildebrand shook her head, as she patted Annie's hand. "No, dear. I'm just so thankful you both came by to see me. I asked Gertie to make sure you knew I wouldn't be home today. She said she would take care of everything."

Dan nodded. "Yes, she called the social worker to let her know what happened. Annie and I need to give you our phone numbers in case of another emergency."

"Excuse me," a nurse said, as she pulled the curtain back. "I'm sorry, but it's time for her medication."

Dan and Annie moved to the other side of the bed. "Mrs. Hildebrand, we better go and let you get some rest. We'll come back tomorrow afternoon," Dan said.

Despite the nurse saying that Mrs. Hildebrand was expected to make a full recovery, Annie felt guilty for leaving her alone. She wondered if Mrs. Hildebrand felt lonely. What if she got scared during the night?

When they left the hospital, Dan said very little during the drive home. He knew how upset Annie had become when he first told her the news. Annie had grown very fond of the elderly lady and vice-versa. They formed a special bond and he wondered if it was attributed to the lack of a motherly influence.

After Dan walked her to the front door and said goodnight, Annie went inside. Her father was sitting at the kitchen table, drinking a cup of hot tea. She sat down in the chair across from him and proceeded to tell him about Mrs. Hildebrand's accident. He continued listening while cutting two pieces of a chocolate cake and placing them onto paper plates. He poured Annie a glass of milk and consoled her by telling her that the hospital was the best place for Mrs. Hildebrand. He assured her that the nurses would keep a close watch on the elderly lady.

After they finished their cake, Annie kissed her father goodnight and headed upstairs. She loved her father for saying all the right things, but she still felt uneasy. As she turned down the covers and started to crawl into bed, she refrained. She slowly lowered herself to her knees and bowed her head. Although she prayed on a regular basis, it had been a while since she knelt beside her bed.

As she whispered amen and lifted her head, she felt like a burden had been lifted. The dark cloud that had followed her from the time she had learned about Mrs. Hildebrand was gone. She could go to sleep with assurance that the elderly lady would return home and revert to her spunky self.

****

The Big Bear Café was crowded as students pushed their way through the busy line, in hopes of finding an empty table. Kim waved across the room as Annie peered through the crowd.

"Oh, thank goodness you got a table," Annie exclaimed, as she slid out a chair.

Kim smiled. "I hope you don't mind, but I went ahead and ordered for us."

"Chicken salad on wheat?" Annie asked.

Kim laughed. "Of course. What else?"

Kim opened the flap on her purse and removed a small envelope. "Look at this," she said. Annie opened the envelope and removed a picture. "Who is this?" she asked, shrugging her shoulders.

Kim raised her eyebrows. "Look again," she remarked.

Annie studied the picture. "I don't know, but it looks creepy."

"It's Jill," Kim remarked.

Annie looked at the picture again. "Jill?"

Kim nodded. "I know, it's pretty amazing."

The picture didn't resemble the young woman she had seen at church. Jill had short black hair and dark makeup that personified a gothic look.

"Wow. That's quite a look," Annie exclaimed.

Kim explained that Jill came from a broken home and started hanging around with the wrong crowd. Her parents claimed they couldn't control her and agreed to send her to reform school. She had made some progress, but it was the time Kim and Darren spent with her that really made a difference. Kim had been taking Jill to the church's youth group meetings and Jill was beginning to make new friends.... good friends.

"I'm trying to show her that a person can be cool without being wild," Kim said.

"Well, whatever you're doing seems to be working," Annie said.

Kim shrugged. "I hope so, but you hear all these horror stories about people falling off the wagon and going back to their old ways. I just hope it doesn't happen with her."

Annie flashed a sincere smile. "Try not to think of what could happen. Be proud of what you and Darren have accomplished with her."

"Yeah. You're right," Kim said. "So what happened with Mrs. Hildemeyer, is it?"

"Hildebrand," Annie corrected. "She lost her balance and fell off her porch. I'm just so glad she didn't break anything." Annie told Kim about Mrs. Hildebrand being in the hospital and how the doctors and nurses expected a full recovery.

Kim rested her cheek in her palm as she listened to her friend. "So how are things with you and Dan?"

Annie shrugged. "Fine. I still don't know anything about his family, though."

Kim lowered her brows. "That's so weird," she said.

Annie nodded. "Yeah, he's very secretive." She held up a finger as she chewed. "He said he would tell me everything, but not right now," she continued.

"Do you believe him?" Kim asked.

Annie sighed. "I have to. I lo...like him."

Kim's eyes widened as she was about to speak.

Embarrassed by what she had almost said, Annie shook her head. "No. Don't go there."

Kim held up her hands. "Okay, okay."

After finishing their lunch, they walked back to campus. It was an unusually warm day and Annie decided to go to the library before her next class. It was too humid to sit in the courtyard.

"I'll call you later," Annie said.

Kim smiled. "Thanks for listening to me go on and on about Jill."

"You don't have to thank me. That's what friends are for," Annie said.

Kim shrugged. "I know, but I just want you to know how much I appreciate it."

Annie flashed a quick smile. "I know. I'll talk to you later."

As Annie walked across the lawn, she heard Kim yell across the courtyard. "Annie!"

Annie turned around and shielded her eyes from the sun. "What?" she yelled.

"It's okay to admit it," Kim yelled.

Annie smiled as she shook her head. "Go to class," she yelled, ignoring her friend's comment.

CHAPTER FIFTEEN

A nnie's father was preparing his lunch when she stumbled into the kitchen. "My goodness, you're up early for a Saturday," he said.

She yawned, as she poured a cup of coffee into a mug. "Yeah. Mrs. Hildebrand gets to come home today."

Her father poured the remainder of the coffee into a thermos. "I'm really proud of you kids." Y'all have really gone above and beyond to help that poor woman."

Annie reached for the creamer. "I feel sorry for her. She doesn't have anyone."

He smiled. "If only your mother could see what a wonderful young woman you have become."

Annie flashed a sympathetic smile. "Well, I have to be honest and tell you that it wasn't easy in the beginning, but I like being around her. She has so many interesting stories."

He laughed. "Oh, I'm sure she does." Glancing at the clock, he grabbed his lunch box and kissed Annie on the cheek. "See you tonight, Hon."

"Bye, Daddy," she said as she placed their dishes in the dishwasher.

Annie spent the next hour getting ready and cleaning out her car. She and Dan decided to take her car to pick up Mrs. Hildebrand since the corvette didn't have a backseat.

It was almost ten o'clock by the time they arrived at the hospital. They could tell Mrs. Hildebrand was anxious to go home. The nurses said she stared out the window for two hours, waiting for them to arrive. Annie helped Mrs. Hildebrand sign the release papers while Dan gathered her belongings.

Mrs. Hildebrand thanked them repeatedly for picking her up. "I hope Gertie tended to my flowers," she remarked.

Annie looked in the rear-view mirror. "She did, Mrs. Hildebrand. Dan and I stopped by your house every day before we came to the hospital. As a matter of fact, Dan has a surprise for you," she said.

Dan smiled and turned around to face the elderly lady. "That's right, Mrs. H. I think you'll really be surprised."

Mrs. Hildebrand leaned forward and patted his shoulder. "I look forward to it."

As they pulled into her driveway, she noticed the painted mailbox. "Oh, my goodness. Just look at that," she said.

Annie smiled. "Well, that's not all, but let's get you into the house and we'll show you the other surprise."

It was obvious that every step was painful, but Mrs. Hildebrand was adamant about seeing her flowers before she went inside. They were just as vibrant as the day she and Annie planted them.

"Well since you're going to be stubborn, we may as well show you this," Annie said, as she pointed to the benches that were once worn and faded.

Mrs. Hildebrand was so excited, she almost lost her balance. "My benches! They are beautiful again."

Annie and Dan enjoyed watching her enthusiasm. "Okay, let's get you inside now," Annie demanded.

As they piled pillows and blankets on her chaise lounge, Mrs. Hildebrand walked into the dining room. A few minutes later she returned with two small presents. "I was going to give these to you on Tuesday," she said.

Looking surprised, Dan and Annie reached for the presents. While Dan tore into his package, Annie carefully removed the pink ribbon that helped secure the wrapping paper.

"No way!" Dan said, as he opened the box.

Annie's mouth dropped, as he carefully removed the beautiful glass figurine from the box.

"It's the doves," he said.

Mrs. Hildebrand's eyes filled with tears as she watched him hold the figurines up to the light.

"Mrs. H., I can't accept this," he said.

She nodded. "Oh, nonsense. I want you to have them," she said.

Dan ran his fingers across the figurines. "I don't know what to say. I know how much these mean to you," he continued.

Mrs. Hildebrand patted his hand. "Enjoy them," she said.

He hesitated before placing them back into the box. "Thank you," he said, as he carefully wrapped the tissue paper around the delicate ornaments.

Mrs. Hildebrand turned her attention toward Annie. "My dear, open yours now," she said.

As Annie opened the package, she gasped. "Oh!" Her hand was shaking as she gently pulled the delicate glass figure from the box. It was a pink and white carriage. Annie threw her arms around Mrs. Hildebrand. "Oh, I love it. I have never seen anything so beautiful in my life," she said.

Mrs. Hildebrand smiled. "I'm delighted. Someday I will give you the missing pieces to complete the collection," she said.

Annie studied the figurine, but couldn't understand what the elderly lady was talking about. Not wanting to appear confused, she simply smiled and thanked her.

Dan and Annie spent the remainder of the afternoon learning more about Mrs. Hildebrand's life. The assignment was beginning to evolve into a historical masterpiece.

Dan cleared his throat. "Mrs. Hildebrand, if you don't mind me asking, when did George pass away?"

There was an awkward silence. He hadn't intended to upset her. "I'm sorry; you don't have to answer that."

Mrs. Hildebrand gazed at the portrait on the wall. "It was nineteen and ninety-two," she answered.

Dan felt guilty for asking, but the assignment required many details to indicate the depth of the interviews.

"That must have been very painful for you," Annie said.

Without taking her eyes from the picture, she nodded. "It was indeed."

Annie stared at the paper, as Dan made sure to capture every word she was speaking.

She offered the elderly lady a sympathetic smile. "I know how you feel. My dad struggles with it every day."

Mrs. Hildebrand reached for Annie's hand. "Such a gentle soul you are. It's a tough thing for a young woman to grow up without her mother." Annie squeezed the lady's hand. "Some days are harder than others, but I try to focus on the memories. That's what keeps me going."

Dan couldn't take his eyes off Annie. She was so innocent and so honest.

Annie loosened her grip and rubbed Mrs. Hildebrand's hand. Her skin was almost transparent, making her veins appear very dark. Annie looked beyond that and stared at the ring. It was so beautiful that it almost camouflaged the lady's imperfections.

"Got it for my twenty-fifth anniversary," Mrs. Hildebrand said.

Annie blushed, knowing it must have been obvious that she was gawking at the ring. "I have never seen such a beautiful ring in my life," she confessed.

Mrs. Hildebrand placed her hand on her chest. "It is and will always be my most treasured possession," she said. "I still remember the night that George gave it to me."

Annie watched the woman's facial expressions, hoping she would reveal more to them. She then turned to make sure Dan was still writing. This was too important to miss. He sensed this and looked up. Their eyes locked for a brief moment.

Annie slowly turned to refocus her attention to Mrs. Hildebrand. "Tell us," she said.

The elderly lady smiled. "Okay, okay. Where was I? Oh, yes, George and I were going to go to dinner that night to celebrate. I bought a red dress for the occasion. Oh, I was a sight back then. A real looker, you know." She smiled and winked at Dan. "I had purchased a gold watch from Stern's, the best jewelry store in town. I had them engrave something special on the back."

"What did it say?" Annie asked.

Dan laughed as he observed Annie's enthusiasm.

Mrs. Hildebrand glanced at the portrait again. "To my darling husband, George. I'll love you forever, Grace."

Annie's mouth dropped open. "Grace," she whispered. They had only known her as Mrs. Hildebrand.

"I was so excited to give him the watch that it never occurred to me he would surprise me with such an extravagant gift." She paused before continuing. "I haven't taken it off since," she confessed.

"Did he give it to you during dinner?" Dan asked.

Mrs. Hildebrand's cheeks turned rosy. "Oh, well, we didn't actually make it to dinner," she said.

Dan laughed. "Did he like the watch?"

Mrs. Hildebrand smiled. "Yes, and he wore it every day until he died." Her smile slowly faded, as her eyes became heavy. They knew she was struggling to stay awake. Dan tapped his watch as he signaled to Annie. Annie nodded and stood up slowly.

"Mrs. Hildebrand," Annie whispered, as she adjusted the pillow.

The elderly lady slowly opened her eyes.

"We better go and let you get some rest. Is there anything you need before we go?" she asked.

"No, dear, I'm fine." she responded.

Dan stood behind Annie as she straightened the blanket.

"Okay, then. We'll come by tomorrow after church and check on you." Annie said.

Mrs. Hildebrand nodded.

"We'll lock the door on the way out," Dan said.

As they backed out of Mrs. Hildebrand's driveway, Dan reached for Annie's hand. "Feel like a movie?" he asked.

Glancing in his direction, she shrugged her shoulders. "Sure. What did you have in mind?"

"I don't know. To be honest, I don't even know what's playing," he confessed.

Annie laughed. "You don't know what's playing, but you want to go to the movies?"

"Okay forget it," he said.

Annie could tell by the tone of his voice that he was embarrassed. "Hey, I was just joking," she said. "A movie sounds great."

Dan shook his head. "Mmmm... Maybe some other time."

As they approached Annie's house, she wondered if he would stay for a while. Without saying a word, he followed her to the front door.

Annie turned to face him. "What do you want to do?" she asked.

With his hands in his pockets, he shrugged.

Annie studied his face, trying to figure out if he was mad or embarrassed. She cleared her throat. "Let's go to the movies like you suggested," she said.

He shook his head while staring at the porch floor. "Nah, let's just stay here."

Annie frowned at her loss for words. "Do you want to sit down?" she asked.

He followed her to the swing, but didn't say a word.

"Look Dan, I...."

As she began to speak, he turned and reached for both of her hands. He pulled her closer to him and gently pressed his lips against hers. As he moved away, he studied her expression.

Her eyes widened as she backed away. He squinted, trying to understand her resistance. "I'm sorry. I don't know what came over me," he confessed.

Annie's heart was racing. She pushed a strand of hair from her face as she tried to regain her composure.

Dan leaned forward and buried his hands into his hair. "Annie... I'm so sorry, I...I'm so sorry," he repeated.

She knew her expression made him feel guilty and ashamed, but he had no reason to be embarrassed. She didn't mean to react that way. It happened so fast that it caught her off guard. Annie playfully elbowed him. "Dan," she whispered.

He leaned back against the swing, but stared straight ahead. He was too embarrassed to look at her.

Annie rubbed his arm. "Hey, it's okay. You have nothing to be sorry about. I was just startled, that's all," she said.

He didn't say a word. Instead, he rubbed his forehead and leaned forward again.

Annie turned toward him. "Please don't feel bad. You didn't do anything wrong," she said.

Dan slowly turned his head until their eyes met. "I should go. You have to get up early in the morning," he whispered.

Annie rubbed his hand and hesitated before speaking. "Are you going with me tomorrow?" she asked.

Dan's mouth curled slightly, as he continued staring into her eyes. He raised his brows. "Do you want me to?" he asked.

Offering a sincere smile, Annie nodded.

As they stood on the edge of the porch steps, Dan pulled her close again, but this time he kissed the crown of her head. She pressed her face into his chest as she heard the faint sound of his heart beating. He held her gently, as he rested his chin on her head.

"I better go," he whispered.

Annie nodded as she looked into his eyes. "Okay."

"See you tomorrow," he said, releasing her from his embrace.

****

Annie was lying in bed, thinking about the kiss they had shared, just an hour before. The old ceiling fan above her bed rattled with every turn. She wondered if Dan was lying in bed thinking about her too.

She replayed the scene repeatedly in her mind and wished she had reacted differently. Annie wanted to call him and confess she was glad it happened. She wanted to tell him she was sorry for appearing so distant. The truth was she had never been kissed like that before. She dated a few boys in high school, but they were more like friends than anyone she really cared about. Dan was special.

She was beginning to have strong feelings for him, but she was afraid at the same time. She knew she had to be cautious because there was so much she didn't know about him. Patience was the key, but how long could she wait? How long did he expect her to be kept in the dark? Annie tossed and turned. She resolved to the fact that it was going to be a sleepless night.

The sound of crickets mimicked a familiar lullaby as she felt her eyes become heavy. The warm air from the window filled her room as her body became relaxed. Her thoughts transformed into dreams. She felt as if she had been asleep for hours when she was suddenly startled. It took her a minute to realize that the phone was ringing.

Annie rolled over and reached for the receiver. "Hello," she moaned. Her heart began to race as she sat up in bed and looked at the clock. It was 10:36 p.m.

"I'm sorry to wake you dear, but I think you should come over here right away," Mrs. Hildebrand said.

Annie's voice was trembling. "Are you okay?" she asked.

"Yes," Mrs. Hildebrand replied calmly. "Annie, please come as soon as possible."

Annie sighed. "Okay, okay, but are you hurt? Do you need an ambulance?" She didn't pay attention to the elderly lady's response. Her mind was racing. She needed to get dressed, call Dan, and wake her father. She knew her father would be worried if he woke up and she was gone.

Annie turned the light on and began to dial. "Oh, what is his number?" she whispered. Realizing Dan's cell phone number was programmed into her phone, she reached for her purse. As she held the phone to her ear, she reached for a pair of jeans. "Come on, Dan, pick up the phone." His greeting came on. She figured he had his phone turned off.

As she frantically got dressed, she imagined Mrs. Hildebrand falling, but not wanting to go back to the hospital. Annie stumbled into her father's room. The flickering screen on the television provided enough light for her to make her way to her father's bed.

"Daddy," wake up. "Mrs. Hildebrand called and asked me to come over," she said.

Her father quickly rolled over. "What is it Honey?" he asked.

"I don't know, she wouldn't tell me. I think she's scared or hurt."

He threw back the covers. "I'll go with you."

She patted his arm. "No, stay here, and I'll call you when I make it," she insisted.

Annie raced through town and became frustrated as she caught every red light. "Come on," she yelled, as she hit the steering wheel with her palm. She repeatedly called Dan, but his voicemail picked up every time.

Mrs. Hildebrand's porch light made it easier for Annie to see the driveway. As she pulled in, she noticed Dan's car. "Oh, thank God!" she said. Maybe Mrs. Hildebrand was talking to him at the same time she was trying to call.

Annie rushed to the front porch, skipping every other step. She could see Mrs. Hildebrand moving toward the door.

"Come in, come in," Mrs. Hildebrand exclaimed.

Annie reached for her arms. "What's wrong?"

Mrs. Hildebrand nodded toward the living room. In a state of confusion, Annie followed behind her. Dan was sitting on the edge of the couch with his head buried in his hands. Annie glanced between him and Mrs. Hildebrand. "I, I.....," Annie stuttered, "What's going on?"

Mrs. Hildebrand motioned toward the chair. "Sit down, Dear," she said.

Annie looked at Dan who remained in the same position. She dropped her purse beside the chair and sat down. She rubbed her eyes, trying to focus on what was taking place.

Mrs. Hildebrand slowly lowered herself onto the couch, beside Dan. She cleared her throat as she moved her hand in a circular motion across his back. "Annie's here now," she whispered.

Annie felt a lump in her throat. She knew something was wrong and the suspense was killing her. She started to speak, but Mrs. Hildebrand held her finger to her lips.

Refusing to look up, Dan shook his head, as he rocked back and forth.

"Dan, Honey, you know you need to talk to her," Mrs. Hildebrand said.

Sitting there in silence, Annie continued staring at Dan. Her mind raced as she tried to speculate why he was upset. She knew it had to be more than the kiss.

"Just give him a minute," the elderly lady whispered. "He pleaded with me not to call you."

Still confused, Annie bit the corner of her lip. She wanted to move closer to him, but she feared how he would react. After all, Mrs. Hildebrand just told her that he didn't want her to come over.

"Dan," Mrs. Hildebrand whispered.

He slowly lifted his head. His face was blood red and his lips were quivering. His cheeks were streaked from the tears that poured from his eyes.

Annie's eyes traced down his cheek as another teardrop fell onto his arm. She leaned forward and rubbed his hand. The sadness in his eyes was breaking her heart. "It's okay," Annie whispered, "I'm here."

Mrs. Hildebrand continued rubbing his back. "Dan, she cares about you. Talk to her."

Dan cut his eyes toward Annie, then looked away, as he clasped his hands together.

Mrs. Hildebrand patted him on the leg. "I'm going to give you some time alone," she said.

Annie watched her move slowly down the hall, until the she could no longer be seen. She felt helpless since she had never seen him like that before. "Dan," she whispered, "Please talk to me."

He crossed his arms and stared toward the empty hallway, refusing to make eye contact with Annie.

She watched his mouth, hoping and praying he would say something. They sat there in silence for what seemed like an eternity. "God please help me say the right thing," she whispered. She sat there for another minute, mentally preparing herself for his reaction.

Annie slowly made her way to the couch and knelt beside him. She watched as another tear rolled down his cheek. She gently brushed her hand across his cheek, wiping the tear from his face. "Please talk to me," she whispered.

He looked up and their eyes met. With her hand still on his cheek, he cupped his hand over hers. Annie's lips formed a warm, sympathetic smile. "Whatever it is, I want to help you."

He lowered her hand to his lips and closed his eyes. "It's so complicated," he said.

"I want to help," she pleaded.

He sighed. "You don't want to get involved with me."

Annie reached for his hands. "Don't say that. Let me help you."

He shook his head. "You can't. Nobody can."

"But why? Why can't you trust me?" she cried.

He squeezed her hands. "This is something I have to figure out," he said.

Annie firmly pulled his hands toward her. "Dan, I can't do this anymore. You're breaking my heart."

He rubbed his thumbs across her hand and looked deep into her eyes. "I'm sorry. I don't mean to hurt you. You have to know that," he confessed.

She sighed, knowing that she couldn't continue this charade. "Dan, every time I feel like there is something between us, you push me away. I don't understand what's going on with you."

He tilted her chin with his hand. "There is something between us. Something very special," he said.

Annie looked into his blue eyes that sparkled in the light. "Then trust me. Confide in me like I have confided in you. You know so much about me, practically everything, and I don't know anything about you or your family," she continued.

Dan stared into her eyes, but it was as if he were looking into her soul, contemplating if he should tell her. "Can we go outside and get some fresh air?" he asked.

Annie followed him onto the porch and watched as the moonlight danced across his face. He gripped the rails as he stared into the darkness. "God knows I want to tell you everything. I came close so many times, but I just couldn't do it," he said. He took a deep breath. "Remember all those times that you got so frustrated with me for not answering my phone?" he asked.

"Yes," Annie whispered.

He hesitated before continuing. "Annie, my life is a mess..... I'm a mess. My home life is nothing like yours. You have a father who cares about you and loves you for who you are." His voice began to quiver as he leaned into the rails. "It's not like that with my family. My dad hates me."

Wrinkles creased across her forehead. "Oh, Dan, I'm sure he doesn't feel that way."

He turned his back away from her and began to cry. "It's true. I heard him talking to my mom. I always knew he felt that way, but lately it has become more obvious. He doesn't even talk to me. Nobody talks to anyone anymore, especially after...."

"After what, Dan?" she asked.

"After Robert died," he whispered.

Annie's mouth dropped open. She felt a chill run up her spine. "Robert?" she whispered.

He nodded. "Yeah, Robert was... my brother."

Annie couldn't believe what she was hearing. Why didn't he tell her he had a brother that passed away? She felt a lump in her throat when she started to speak. "I don't know what to say," she said.

He turned around, pressing his back into the post. "Robert had everything going for him. You would have liked him a lot. He was my hero and everyone looked up to him," he said, wiping away another tear.

"What happened to him?" Annie asked softly.

Dan swallowed hard. "Eight months ago Robert was studying for the bar exam. My Dad was so proud that he was following in his footsteps and he had so many dreams of them working together. Dad was going to hire him and change the name of his firm to Wilson & Wilson. He ordered custom furniture for Robert's office. I don't think I have ever seen my father so happy in all his life," Dan said.

Annie leaned forward, cupping her hands together. Her expression begged him to continue.

Dan let out a deep sigh as he crossed his arms. "Robert needed to blow off some steam, you know, from the endless nights of cramming, so we grabbed our surfboards and headed to the beach. Robert was a great surfer." Dan smiled. "I remember one competition when he beat out twenty guys. "Man, you should have seen him. He was unbeatable." Dan's smile slowly faded as he continued. "Anyway, we met up with some of our friends and hit the waves. We were having a blast."

Annie glanced up as he stopped talking. She wanted to provide some comforting words,
but she refrained. He needed a minute.

Dan turned away from her, resting his arm on the post. "We decided to walk down the beach and find a less crowded area." He sighed. "That's when it happened. We heard a cry from the water, but the waves made it too difficult to see where it was coming from. All of a sudden, we spotted a boy who was struggling to keep his head above the water. He was in very deep water, almost to the second sandbar. My brother and one of his friends took off after the boy. The waves were rough and we watched from the shore as my brother grabbed the boy."

Annie's throat tightened, as tears poured from her eyes. "What happened?" she asked.

Dan's voice became hoarse as he sobbed. "His mother was frantically screaming and pointing. I can still hear her cries." "My baby. Somebody help my baby."

Annie struggled to control her emotions. She had to be strong for Dan, but it was difficult to listen to him relive that horrible incident. She remained silent as he continued.

"We watched as Robert and his friend swam toward the shore with the boy. They struggled against the current. All I remember was watching the white caps of the large waves rolling behind them. Robert's friend and the boy surfaced, but.....," He paused as his voice quivered.

Annie cupped her hand over her mouth as she visualized the terrible scene. "He drowned?" she asked.

Dan nodded. "Yeah, but do you want to know what's so weird?" he asked.

Annie raised her eyebrows.

"Even after eight months, I still look for him. I know it sounds crazy, but I expect him to walk through the door," Dan said.

Annie nodded. "It's not crazy. I do the same thing. I still fantasize my mom will be in the kitchen cooking when I get home or working in her flower beds."

Dan looked down. "It's hard enough having to deal with this unbearable pain, but I feel like I lost my parents too. It's like they died with him."

Annie's heart ached for Dan, but at the same time, she felt sympathy for his parents. "Have you told your parents how you feel?" she asked.

Dan snickered sarcastically. "Annie, you don't understand. My Dad goes to the office every day, then he comes home and locks himself in the study. Mom stayed in bed for six months, night and day, sobbing into her pillow. Now she stays busy from the time she gets up until she goes to bed."

"You need to talk to them," she said.

He shook his head. "No! That's just it. They won't talk about it. I have tried. Jen, my sister, has tried, but they are in denial," he continued.

Annie was at a loss for words and this frustrated her. She found it ironic that she was majoring in Sociology, yet she couldn't offer any comforting words. As they stood there in silence, Annie reflected on her mother's death and remembered how the pain consumed her. She understood what Dan was going through.

"Dan," she whispered, "I know it may not be much of a consolation right now, but trust me when I say that time heals all pain. You have to put your faith in God and lean on family and friends."

He stared into her eyes, studying the warmth of her expression. "I feel so alone," he confessed.

Annie moved closer to him. Her heart was beating rapidly. Without hesitation, she wrapped her arms around his neck and rubbed the back of his head. "You're not alone," she whispered.

Dan pulled her closer. She could hear his heart beating as they stood there in complete silence, holding one another for a long time. "Are you okay?" she whispered.

Dan stared into her eyes, refusing to look away. "I tried so hard, for so long, pretending things were okay when in reality, I felt like I was dying inside."

"Why didn't you tell me?" she asked.

Dan sighed. "It's embarrassing, Annie. Don't you think I'm ashamed that I haven't been able to take you to my house? It was easier to avoid the conversation than take a chance on...," he paused. "Like I said, my parents are nothing like your Dad."

Annie reached for his hands. "You have nothing to be ashamed of."

He knew she was sincere, but he still felt embarrassed. "That's sweet of you to say," he said.

It was getting late and Annie knew her father would be worried, but she didn't want to leave Dan, not in this condition. He sensed this and stroked her arms as he cleared his throat. "Listen, I'm going to drive you home, then come back here. Mrs. H. said I could stay here for a few days. I need some time away from home to figure things out," he said.

Annie shook her head. "You don't have to drive me home. I'll be fine."

Dan held up his finger. "No. It's late and I'm going to drive you home. Just wait here a second. I'm going to let her know that I'm taking you home and I'll be back."

Very few words were spoken in the car. It had been a long, emotional night. The clock on the radio read 1:25 a.m. As they made their way toward the front door, they remained silent. All of the lights were off inside the house. The porch light provided ample lighting for her to rummage through her purse for the keys.

"Found them," she said with a smile.

Dan smiled as he stared into her eyes. "Thank you," he whispered.

"For what?" Annie asked.

"For listening and being so understanding."

She raised her eyebrows. "Thank you for telling me. I know how hard it was for you."

As they continued looking into each other's eyes, Dan gently brushed the side of her face with his hand. Without speaking a word, she read his lips as he mouthed the words, "I love you."

****

Annie pulled her pillow close, smiling as she reflected on those three little words he had revealed. Was it true? Did he really say it or did she just imagine it? It was hard for her to believe he could love her. She never pictured herself with someone as good looking as Dan. She felt inferior at times, but he had told her on more than one occasion that she was beautiful. Why couldn't she believe him? After all, she had caught him staring at her so many times.

Her smile quickly faded, as she thought about the pain he was going through. She wanted so desperately to help him, but how? How could she help him mend his relationship with his parents? She glanced at the clock, realizing it was too late to call Kim, but she needed her. Annie knew she wouldn't have an opportunity to talk to Kim at church. Her mind raced as she tried to figure out what to do. If she called her on the cell phone, it wouldn't wake her parents.

The longer she lay in bed, the more convinced she was that she had to talk with her. Annie winced as she pressed the send button. Five rings later, she was relieved to hear her friend's voice.

"Hello," Kim groaned in a raspy voice.

"Kim, I'm sorry to call so late, but I really need to talk," Annie confessed.

"Mmmmm. What's up?" she groaned.

"He finally told me what was going on. You're not going to believe it," she said.

Kim listened as Annie told her about Dan's brother and how his family life was in shambles.

"Oh, Kim, you should have seen him tonight. It was heartbreaking."

"Wow! I can't believe it. He seemed so together," Kim mumbled.

"I know. I'm still in shock, but you can't say anything to him. When you see him tomorrow, act like you don't know."

"Okay, okay," Kim promised.

Annie sighed. "Um, there's something else."

"What?" Kim asked.

Annie felt a sweet sensation sweep through her. "He um... He told me he loved me," she whispered.

"What?" Kim shrieked.

Annie held the phone away from her ear. She was sure everyone in Kim's house must have heard her.

"Oh, my gosh. When? What did you say?" Kim asked.

Annie smiled. "Tonight. He kind of whispered it."

"And?" Kim asked.

"And what?" Annie asked.

"Did you say it back?" she asked.

Annie sighed. "No, but I really didn't have time to react," she confessed.

After a few seconds of silence, Kim cleared her throat. "Do you love him?"

Annie pulled her pillow closer. "Yeah, I think I do," she said.

"Ohhhh, I'm so happy for you, Annie."

Annie bit the corner of her lip. "Kim, can I ask you a question?"

"Of course."

Annie hesitated.

"What?" Kim asked.

"I was just wondering if it's embarrassing to say it."

Kim's voice softened. "No, you will know when the time is right and you will want to say it."

After they hung up, Annie thought about what Kim said. She felt butterflies in her stomach. As she remembered the look on his face, she pulled the covers over her shoulders. "I love you too Dan," she whispered in the darkness.

CHAPTER SIXTEEN

Annie sat on the window seat in her room and pulled back the curtains, just enough to allow light to peek through. The sun almost blinded her. She wrapped her arms around her knees as she watched the man next door walking down the driveway in his robe. She saw him wave to her father before he bent down to pick up the paper. Her eyes shifted down to see her father.

Annie released the curtains, hoping he wouldn't look toward her window. Her palms became sweaty. What was she going to tell him about last night? She knew honesty had always been very important between them, but she wasn't comfortable talking to him about what happened at Mrs. Hildebrand's house.

Annie paced back and forth, trying to build up enough courage to go downstairs. She knew she had to face her father and she would rather do it now than when Dan arrived. She was afraid her father would ask about last night and this would make Dan feel uncomfortable. Annie let out a deep breath as she opened the door. She cringed as the stairs squeaked below her feet.

Her father was sitting in the recliner reading the newspaper, as she turned the corner.

"Is that you Honey?"

Annie squeezed her eyes shut. "Yes, sir," she answered.

He folded the paper and placed it on the arm of the chair, waiting for her to walk in the room.

She slowly made her way into the living room. "Morning," she said, as she stood beside his chair.

He patted the arm of the chair. "Is Mrs. Hildebrand okay?" he asked.

She plopped down on the chair, as she bit her lip. "Uh huh."

He removed his glasses. "Well, what was wrong?"

Annie forced a smile and patted him on the shoulder. "Oh, nothing...really. She was just scared."

Her father rubbed his chin as he studied her expression. "I see. And where is your car?" he asked.

Annie's eyes widened and she swallowed hard. "My car? Um..., at Mrs. Hildebrand's house. I, well, Dan brought me home since it was so late," she said, letting out a deep breath.

He continued stroking his chin, as the wrinkles in his forehead became more defined. "Dan was there?" he asked.

Annie's heart began to pound rapidly, but all she could do was force a nod.

Her father sighed. "Annie, you know that I trust you completely, but you also know how I feel about you being out so late."

Annie frowned. "I know Daddy, but she needed me."

He raised his brows. "Honey, I know and I'm proud of you for being such a good person,
but it doesn't change the fact that it's dangerous."

Annie crossed her arms. "Is that it or is it because you don't trust Dan?"

His temples pulsated as he cut his eyes toward her. "Look, this has nothing to do with trust. I'm your father and I love you, but I don't want you on the road that late regardless of who is driving."

Annie glanced away from him. She knew deep down he wasn't being unreasonable and that he loved her more than anything.

"Do I make myself clear?" he asked.

She nodded. "Yes sir."

Annie went upstairs and got ready for church. She rushed to get ready before Dan had an opportunity to knock on the door. She knew he would give Dan the same speech he gave her and she didn't want to take that chance.

As she made her way downstairs, she noticed her father was no longer in the living room. She breathed a sigh of relief as she heard water running in his bathroom. She peeked through the window and saw Dan turning in the driveway. She glanced at herself in the hall mirror and smoothed her dress before opening the door. With her Bible in one hand, she nervously gripped her purse strap with the other. Her palms were sweaty. She felt as if her mind was racing out of control. *I wonder if he remembers what he said. I wonder if he expected me to say it back. I wonder if he knows I read his lips.*

"Hi," he said, with a bashful grin.

Surprisingly, he looked well rested and refreshed. His eyes were no longer red and his face didn't reflect any sign of turmoil.

Her stomach ached at the thought of him mentioning what happened. She wasn't ready to talk about it yet. She had to say something quickly. "Sleep well?"

He shrugged his shoulders. "Not really, but I did a lot of thinking."

Annie smiled, but her mind was preoccupied with the conversation she had with her father. She tried to pretend nothing was wrong because the last thing she wanted was for Dan to find out her father was upset. *Just look at him... So beautiful, but so troubled.* He didn't need another issue to worry about.

Annie was hopeful that church would provide Dan with a sense of peace. After she lost her mother, she found solace in being surrounded by the love she felt in church. She hoped her father would yearn for that feeling again. She missed him being there with her.

As she sat on the pew, her mind drifted back to her mother's funeral. She looked toward the altar and thought about the irony of how her mother's casket was in the very place that provided her so much comfort.

"Isn't that wonderful?" Kim remarked.

Annie jumped. "I'm sorry, what did you say?" she asked.

Kim frowned. "Are you okay?" she whispered.

Annie nodded, as she curled her index finger over her lip. She wondered if Dan noticed her pensive demeanor too. Her mind was plagued with so many emotions. She had to pull herself together.

Kim studied Annie's expression. "I said Jill will be singing in the youth choir this morning. Are you sure you're okay?"

Annie's lips formed a partial smile. "Yes, I'm fine," she whispered. "I'm excited about Jill."

As they sat on the pew watching and listening to Jill and the other teenagers sing, Kim smiled proudly. Jill had made such an improvement in a short amount of time. Her transformation was a true testament to the hard work that Kim and Darren invested in helping the poor girl.

After the service, Annie and Dan hugged Jill and raved about the singing. The teenager flashed a shy smile, as she stood between Kim and Darren. They continued talking for a few minutes, waving to the other church members as they drove away. Kim put her arm around Jill. "Well, we better go if we're going to make the two o'clock matinee."

As they walked their separate ways, Dan elbowed Annie. "Are you up for the lake?" he asked.

Annie's eyes widened as she wondered if he wanted to be alone with her to talk about what happened on her front porch. She hoped the conversation would revolve around his parents. Although she readily admitted to herself that she loved him, she wasn't ready to admit it to him.

On the way to the lake, Dan fidgeted with the radio. Annie could tell he was just as nervous as she was. "Here, pick one out," he said, handing her a CD case.

She flipped through his impressive collection. "Wow, how did you ever collect so many?" she asked.

He smiled as he glanced between her and the road. "I have to admit that I'm a bit of a music junkie."

She smiled. "How about this?"

He nodded. "Yeah, they're awesome," he said. Neither one considered the fact that the CD was comprised of several upbeat songs about falling in love.

Annie thought it was cute the way Dan pretended to play the drums on the steering wheel. He knew all of the words to every song they listened to, but he didn't offer to look her way. She knew it might be too awkward.

They stopped by a local deli and picked up two daily specials. The blanket that Annie had brought on the first picnic was still in Dan's trunk. As they walked hand-in-hand to their familiar shaded spot, Dan remained quiet, but relaxed. He felt comfortable at the lake. Being away from family and Mrs. Hildebrand allowed them to talk more freely.

Annie twirled a stick between her fingers. The words from the song played in her mind. She had heard the song so many times on the radio, but never paid much attention to the lyrics until today. She glanced at Dan, wondering if he related the song to them. Part of her wanted to talk about what had happened, but on the other hand, she hoped he wouldn't bring it up. She needed more time to prepare for that conversation.

"Well, here we are," he said.

Annie grinned. "Yep, here we are."

Dan spread the blanket across the grass. As they enjoyed every bite of their sandwiches, they watched the boats speed across the water.

Dan glanced at Annie. "It's not too late to run away from me, you know."

Annie smiled. "Nah, I don't have the energy to run."

He shook his head and grinned. "You're something else, you know that?"

Without saying a word, she playfully shrugged her shoulders.

He moved closer to her, as they pressed their backs into a tree. His smile faded and his mouth transformed into a serious expression. Rubbing his thumb across her hand, he met her gaze. "You know I wouldn't be mad if you didn't want to have anything to do with me after the assignment," he said.

Annie looked surprised. "Why would you say that?" she asked.

He shrugged. "I don't know. I have a lot of issues to work out, and I wouldn't want you to feel obligated."

Annie held his stare. "You think I'm here because I feel obligated?"

He looked away. His expression said it all.

"Dan," I'm here because I want to be with you, not because I feel obligated."

He raised his eyebrows. "Really?"

She nodded. "Yes, really."

He glanced toward the boats. "I hope you know how much that means to me," he said.

Annie tilted her head to the side. "I want to help you in any way that I can."

He pulled her hand to his lips. "You already have....more than you could ever imagine."

She continued studying his expression, wondering what he meant.

Shaking his head, he formed a half smile. "I don't know how a guy like me got so lucky to find someone like you."

Annie playfully nudged his shoulder. "Yeah, I feel the same way," she said.

Dan snickered. "You don't know how a guy like me got so lucky either, huh?"

She squinted. "You know what I meant."

His smile faded into a serious expression. "Mmmm. Maybe you should tell me," he said.

Annie flashed a nervous smile, as she rubbed the back of her neck.

He raised his eyebrows and gave her a sheepish grin. "You know, you should practice what you preach," he said.

Annie looked up. "And what exactly does that mean?"

He was silent for a minute. His hand felt clammy, as he continued rubbing her hand. "Well, it's um, ironic that you said I was the one who always kept things inside, and you were the open book. That's true except when it comes to your feelings about me." His chest deflated, as he let out a deep breath.

Annie felt a sudden rush of heat run through her body. She hated the fact that she embarrassed easily. How could she respond? Although she knew there was truth in what he said, she struggled to find the right words. She wished she could snap her fingers and disappear.

Realizing he made her feel uncomfortable, he gently elbowed her. "Hey, it's okay. You don't have to tell me. We can talk about something else."

Annie closed her eyes. She knew she owed it to him to tell him that she was falling in love with him. Why was it so hard to say? Didn't he know? Kim said she would know when the time was right and she would want to say it. Her mouth felt dry. If now was the right time, why was she so scared?

She straightened her posture and cleared her throat. "Dan, that's not true. I told you how I felt," she said.

Not wanting to make her feel uncomfortable again, he stared straight ahead. "Well, you told me you cared about me, but you get so tense every time I get near you. I'm getting mixed signals." He wanted to hear her say those words, but he didn't want to pressure her. After all, he wasn't completely convinced that she did love him.

Annie's throat tightened. She felt as though she could hear the rhythm of her heart beating. "I feel the same way you do," she said.

Not wanting to push the issue further, he simply smiled. He hoped she would say it soon.

Dusk was approaching fast. The muggy day surrendered to a cool breeze that felt invigorating, as they drove back to her house with the windows down. They walked hand in hand to the front porch, but neither of them spoke a word. As they stood facing each other, Dan pulled her close, but not as close as he did the night before. "I hope I didn't make you feel uncomfortable," he said.

Annie glanced into his eyes then looked away. "No, I'm fine," she said.

He tried to read her expression, but he couldn't determine if she was being honest. "Okay," he whispered, "I better go and let you get some sleep."

Annie looked up. "Are you going back to Mrs. Hildebrand's house?"

"Yeah," he whispered.

Annie hesitated before speaking. "Are you going to talk to your parents?"

He sighed. "I don't know. I need some more time to figure things out." His embrace became stronger, as he buried his cheek in her hair.

"Dan," she whispered.

"Hmmm," he said.

She remained silent.

He pulled away and looked into her eyes, wondering what she was going to say.

She shook her head. "Never mind." Her heart began to pound rapidly.

He raised his eyebrows. "What?" he asked.

Her eyes widened. "I... forgot what I was going to say," she remarked.

Dan couldn't hide the disappointment on his face. Was she about to tell him she loved him? Why couldn't she say it? After all, she said she felt the same way. He offered a fake smile, as he rubbed her arms. "I better go," he reiterated.

Annie looked into his eyes, wondering if she caused him more confusion. He was right. She was sending mixed signals. She felt a sinking feeling in her stomach, as she watched him get into his car.

****

Annie's father was paying bills at the table when she walked into the kitchen. His eyes glanced over the top of his glasses. "You're home early," he remarked.

Annie leaned against the doorway. "Yeah..., I'm really sorry about last night," she said.

He nodded. "I know."

Annie poured a glass of milk and sat down beside her father. He seemed oblivious to her company, as he stuffed checks into envelopes. Annie ran her finger around the rim of the glass. "Daddy, can I talk to you for a minute?" she asked.

Her father looked up and studied the nervous expression on her face. "Of course, Honey," he said, as he removed his glasses.

She took another sip of milk. "Daddy, I… wasn't totally honest with you about Mrs. Hildebrand."

Her father leaned in, resting his arms on the table. "Oh," he said.

Annie saw the apprehension in his face. "The truth is she asked me to come over because she was concerned about Dan."

His forehead wrinkled as he tried to understand what she was saying. "Why was she concerned about Dan?" he asked.

Annie frowned. "Oh, Daddy, it's complicated. Dan has had a very difficult time lately and Mrs. Hildebrand felt that I should be there," she said. Tears filled her eyes as she told her father everything Dan had disclosed about his life. Annie could tell by the look on her father's face he was concerned as well. She knew she could confide in him and that he would understand. He was the most gentle and patient person she had ever known.

"Is there anything we can do to help?" he asked.

Annie shook her head. "I don't think so. He said he needs time to figure things out. Please don't let him know I told you. He is so ashamed."

He patted her hand. "You'll let me know if there is anything I can do," he said. Annie smiled. "Thanks, Daddy."

Annie got up from the table and rinsed her glass. For a moment he was taken by surprise at how much she resembled her mother. "Annie, can I ask you a question?"

She turned around. "Yeah, sure."

He rubbed the stubble on his chin, as he cleared his throat. "You and Dan….you're pretty serious, huh?" he asked.

Annie's eyes widened. She knew it must have been obvious, but she felt awkward talking to her father about her feelings for Dan. "We enjoy spending time together," she said.

He rested his chin on his knuckles. "You have the same look in your eyes that your Mother had when we fell in love."

Annie twirled her hair as she flashed a shy smile. "Did you know when Mamma first fell for you?" she asked.

He smiled. "I thought I did, but it was nice to hear it."

Annie nodded. She knew her father was right. Dan needed to hear it, too. She kissed her father on the cheek. "I better get ready for bed," she said.

Annie went upstairs and changed into her pajamas. She thought about what her father said and knew she had to tell Dan how she felt. He deserved to hear the truth.

CHAPTER SEVENTEEN

Annie spent most of the morning in the library. She knew she wouldn't have an opportunity to talk with Dan until later that evening. Mondays were usually hectic and their schedules didn't allow them any time to see each other during the day. As she perused through the shelves, a poetry book caught her attention. She nervously glanced over the book at least three times before she removed it from the shelf. It was titled "Poems of Love." She looked around the room to make sure Dan was nowhere in sight.

She read the first two poems as she stood in the aisle. Not completely convinced, she hesitated before taking the book to a nearby table. As she read some of the poems, she thought about how romantic and precise the words were. It was amazing to her that someone could create such a masterpiece of lyrical precision. *That's it. I'll write him a poem.* It seemed like a good idea, but she convinced herself that she would never be able to make the words rhyme.

As she continued glancing through the book, she was struck with another idea. "A letter," she whispered. That was something she could do and it would allow her to dispel any doubts he had. She replaced the book and decided that it would be better to sit in the courtyard to write the letter. Despite the fact the library was a place to escape, students often used it as a place to congregate socially.

Annie walked across the plush green lawn and took a seat on an iron bench. As she removed a piece of notebook paper, she looked around once more to ensure she had complete privacy. "Good," she said. He would never find her out here.

"Dear Dan," she whispered, as she held the pen to the paper. She twisted her mouth and sighed at the difficulty she experienced in starting the letter. "Dear Dan," she whispered again.

She sat there in utter frustration, clicking the pen open and closed. She found it hard to believe that she couldn't write one single word. Now she realized how hard it must have been for him to write her a letter. "Okay," she mumbled, "I'm going to just start writing. I don't have to give it to him if it sounds stupid."

The sound of the bell caught her off guard. She glanced at her watch with a frown. Unfortunately, she had written very little, but decided she would finish later that night, after they went to Mrs. Hildebrand's house. It would have been nice to give him the letter when he dropped her off, but this was something that required time. She wanted the words to be perfect, just like the poems she had read.

Annie was waiting on the front porch when Dan arrived. She was disappointed that she had not been able to complete the letter, but she would work on it later. Annie smiled, as he reached for her hand, and led her to the car. They continued holding hands and talking on the way to Mrs. Hildebrand's house.

Mrs. Hildebrand welcomed Annie with a hug and kiss on the cheek. She was dressed in white pants, a red blouse, and the beautiful broach she had worn when they first met her.

Annie slowly released her embrace. "Wow, you look pretty," Annie said.

Mrs. Hildebrand smoothed the side of her hair. "Gertie and I had our hair appointments today. We go every week, you know."

Annie smiled, as she glanced over her shoulder at Dan. He grinned as he gave her a subtle wink.

Mrs. Hildebrand grabbed Annie's hand and guided her into the living room. "I've got something to show you," she said.

Dan leaned down and whispered in Annie's ear. "Yeah and she refused to let me see it.

She said I would have to be patient and wait for you," he chuckled.

"He's very impatient you know," Mrs. Hildebrand said, without turning around.

Dan shrugged his shoulders and laughed.

Mrs. Hildebrand pointed to the couch. "Here, here, sit down."

They watched her open a black weathered trunk. Her frail body leaned over as she removed several photo albums from the chest. "I thought you might enjoy looking through these. It may help you with your assignment," she said.

Annie and Dan smiled as she placed the albums on the coffee table. The pictures were spilling out of the books and Annie remembered that Mrs. Hildebrand wanted them to arrange her photo albums. Annie was eager to look at the pictures, but she didn't want to spend the entire evening arranging the books.

Mrs. Hildebrand resembled a child at Christmas and couldn't wait for them to open the first album. As she described every picture, Annie made some notes in their journal. The pictures were ideal for their assignment because it allowed them to understand the elderly woman's life. Dan suggested they arrange a collage of pictures to present to Mr. Riley, along with the essay. This would surely guarantee an "A."

"Ohhhh, look," Annie shrieked, as she stared at Mrs. Hildebrand's wedding picture. "You looked so beautiful."

Mrs. Hildebrand's face radiated enthusiasm. "Yes, yes and look at what a sight George was," she said, pointing to the picture.

Annie nodded. "Tell us about your wedding day."

Mrs. Hildebrand folded her hands together and leaned back in the chair. "It was a beautiful day. George looked so handsome and I almost fainted when Daddy walked me down the aisle." She laughed. "I was young and naïve, but, very much in love."

Annie leaned forward, carefully taking in every word that Mrs. Hildebrand had spoken.

"Were you nervous about getting married?" Annie asked.

Mrs. Hildebrand placed her hand over her chest. "Yes, but George was such a gentleman and I knew he would take care of me."

"I love this one," Annie said, pointing to a faded 8x10 picture. It had to be the most romantic picture she had ever seen. George was holding Mrs. Hildebrand's tiny waist as she rested her arms on his strong shoulders. They were looking into each other's eyes and their faces were drawn close together. Annie imagined that it was taken just before they shared the infamous husband and wife kiss.

"May I?" Dan asked, reaching for the picture.

Their eyes locked, as she handed him the picture. For a brief moment, Annie wondered what her wedding would be like. She imagined herself standing across from Dan as he slipped a wedding band on her finger. They would look into each other's eyes and become bonded together by God's love. *Love,* Annie thought. *I'm dreaming about love when I'm having to resort to telling him in a letter. How pathetic.*

After hearing Mrs. Hildebrand talk about her love for George, Annie felt compelled to tell Dan. She had to speak those words to him because he deserved to hear it from her lips rather than having to read it in a letter. She made up her mind. She was going to tell him...tonight.

They spent the next two hours going through old photographs. It was getting late and Dan was anxious to be alone with Annie. Spending the last couple of nights at Mrs. Hildebrand's house allowed him to think and put things in perspective. His anger and pain weren't as strong. He attributed this to being away from the negative energy he felt in his own home. Part of him longed to see his parents, but not yet. He needed a little more time.

He thought about Annie too. His heart ached when he was away from her. He was falling deeper in love with her and this scared him. He knew she cared about him, what if she didn't share the same deep feelings he did? Telling her that he loved her was the truth, but this left him vulnerable.

As he drove her home that night, he reached for her hand. She seemed unusually quiet. He wondered if she felt awkward because of their conversation at the lake. When they pulled into her driveway, he removed his seat belt and turned to face her. It was dark, but the porch light provided enough light to see her face. He leaned his head against the seat. "Do you mind if we talk out here?"

Annie nodded. "Okay," she whispered.

Dan looked into her eyes and squeezed her hand. He found himself enveloped in awkward silence. He reached over and tilted her chin toward him. "Penny for your thoughts."

Annie forced a smile. "Just thinking," she said.

He brushed a strand of hair from her face. "Yeah, I've been doing quite a bit of that lately too," he said.

She raised her eyebrows. "About your parents?"

He paused before answering. "That... among other things."

Annie studied his expression. "Have you decided when you're going home?"

He shook his head. "Mmmm, not yet, but I feel better about the situation."

She flashed a smile. "That's good."

His throat tightened. "Do you want to know what else I've been thinking about?" he asked.

She hesitantly nodded.

"About you, about us," he said.

Annie squirmed in the seat, trying to get comfortable. "Me too," she whispered.

Dan lifted her chin. "Annie, I know this makes you feel uneasy, and God knows that I want you to be comfortable around me, but I need to know how you really feel. I can't hide my feelings, not when it comes to you." He let out a deep breath and hesitated before continuing. "I'm pretty sure you read my lips the other night," he said.

Her eyes widened. This was the moment of truth and she had to tell him, but her stomach tightened.

He ran his fingers through his hair and rubbed his knees, nervously. "Do you know what I said?" he asked.

She bit the side of her lip and nodded.

"It's true," he whispered, "I'm in love with you."

A thousand thoughts raced through her mind, but she froze again. If the time was right, why couldn't she say it?

He stared at her, waiting for a reaction, but she remained speechless. Her silence pained him. His suspicions were confirmed; she didn't love him. He hated himself for admitting it to her. Thankfully, the assignment would be over in three days and they wouldn't be forced to face each other every day. He looked away. "You better get inside," he said.

Annie felt like her heart was going to jump out of her chest. "Dan, I... want you to know that I." She took a deep breath, but she said nothing else.

He bit the side of his cheek, determined not to reveal any more of his feelings. "Annie, please go inside." His voice was low, but firm.

She fought back the tears. *I'm such a fool. What's wrong with me?* She cleared her throat. "Dan," she whispered.

He sighed. "Annie, just go. Please. I need to go," he whispered.

Tears flowed from her eyes as she slowly opened the car door. She wanted him to stop her, but he didn't. As she walked toward the porch, she turned around, hoping he would get out of the car. Instead, she watched as he backed out of the driveway and raced away. She could tell by the loud shifting of gears that he was upset.

CHAPTER EIGHTEEN

The remainder of the week passed by slowly. Dan was very distant in class and for the first time in eight weeks, they didn't spend their afternoons and evenings together. Annie's father knew that something was wrong, but she denied it by telling him they were busy writing their individual essays.

The assignment would be completed on Thursday. Annie sighed. That sounded so final. Although she knew her friendship with Mrs. Hildebrand would continue, she knew she had blown things with Dan.

She cried herself to sleep thinking about how much she hurt him. She desperately needed to talk to Kim, but Darren was always with her. She was certain they were working on their essay too or spending time with Jill. Annie didn't begrudge Kim though because Jill had come so far.

Tears rolled down Annie's cheek as she reflected on the last two months. Dan made her feel special and so alive. She had always wanted to find someone like him, but now she felt alone. The need to talk with someone consumed her, but she had nobody. She couldn't talk to Mrs. Hildebrand because Dan was staying at her house.

Annie picked up the picture frame on her nightstand and ran her finger across the silhouette of her mother. She cried out in agony. Tears spilled onto the glass as her body began to shake. "Oh, Mamma, I miss you so much. What should I do?"

Annie fell asleep with the picture resting on her chest. She awoke to the sound of rain thumping against the gutter. As she focused her eyes on the clock, she was surprised to see that it was only eleven o'clock. She felt as though she had slept all night. As she placed the picture back on the nightstand, her eyes were drawn to her notebook. Now that her eyes were fully focused, she glanced at the clock again. It was 11:02 p.m. Although she couldn't explain it, she woke up feeling different. Her fears about love weren't as prevalent. She sat up in bed and propped her notebook against her knees. She knew deep down that it was probably over, but he was going to know how she felt. She was going to write the letter.

****

The classroom was completely chaotic, as students scrambled to make last minute changes to their assignments. Dan was already seated at the table when Annie arrived, but he barely acknowledged her. She glanced toward him and noticed he had neatly arranged a collage of pictures they had chosen to present.

Annie wanted to spend more time with Mrs. Hildebrand, but it was difficult, considering the fact that Dan was staying at her house. She wondered if Mrs. Hildebrand suspected anything. After all, she was very perceptive for her age.

Mr. Riley entered the classroom. "Take your seats please. We have a lot to do today." He held a stack of papers in his hand. "I will be passing out evaluations. When I call your names, you will be expected to read your essays in front of the class and everyone else will evaluate your assignment."

Annie glanced at the evaluation. It contained several questions, each containing four boxes to be checked. She suddenly felt nervous about presenting in front of the class and hoped Dan would offer to read it.

"Annie Carver and Dan Wilson," Mr. Riley said.

As they stood side-by-side in front of the classroom, Annie observed Dan's expressions as he read their assignment. He looked extremely handsome. He was wearing a light blue oxford shirt with the sleeves rolled up and khaki pants. She could smell the familiar scent of his cologne. It was as if she was seeing him for the first time. She still found it hard to believe that someone of his caliber was interested in her. *Was interested*, she thought. Hopefully, the letter would repair what she had broken. After all, she poured her heart and soul into it and even if he didn't want to reconcile, she wanted him to know how she felt.

Annie listened to the sincerity in his voice as he read the last paragraph of their essay.

This assignment not only afforded us the opportunity to gain an understanding of the elderly, but it also provided us with a gift that we would forever cherish — a friendship. We are honored to call Mrs. Hildebrand our friend. She shared her life stories with us, some joyous, some sad, but above all, she taught us that real love never dies. Not even death can take away the love we carry in our hearts.

To their surprise, all of the students stood up and applauded. Some of the girls were wiping tears from their eyes. The countless hours of studying and working on the assignment paid off.

"Well done!" Mr. Riley said as he applauded with the students. "This is what I hope you will take from this class and apply to your profession."

179

Dan turned toward Annie. His lips formed a forced smile, but he said nothing. She wanted to reach out and hug him, but he turned around and walked away.

When the bell rang, Annie rushed to the table to retrieve her purse. She took a deep breath and removed the letter from her purse. "Please God, let this work," she prayed. Her heart became frantic as she looked around the room. He was gone. She searched the halls, but he was gone.

She ran toward the parking lot and caught a glimpse of him turning onto the main street. "No!" she yelled. "Come back!" As he sped away, she stood there alone. The smell of the previous night's rain permeated through the air, making the humidity unbearable.

CHAPTER NINETEEN

"Can we please talk?" Annie whispered, as she typed a text message. Afraid that she would miss his reply, she held the phone with one hand and she gripped the steering wheel with the other. Her eyes shifted from the road to the phone, but no reply. She looked at the clock, but only two minutes had passed. "Come on, Dan. Please answer," she said. She opted to send a text message because she felt it would be easier to read his rejection than to hear it.

Five more minutes had passed. She wondered if he was purposely ignoring her or he had his phone turned off. The closer she got to Mrs. Hildebrand's house, the more she felt nauseated.

She rehearsed what she would say to him. "Hi! I'm ready to admit it now," she said.

No, that sounds ridiculous. "Dan, I know I was a fool, but please read this letter. It will explain everything." *Good grief. That doesn't sound good, either.* She knew that her phone was turned on, but she felt the need to check it again. By this time, ten minutes had passed and nothing.

As she caught a glimpse of Mrs. Hildebrand's house, she felt sick. Dan's car wasn't in the driveway, but he sometimes parked in the garage. She felt completely numb. Her head pounded and her heart ached, but she remained in her car for a minute, trying desperately to gain enough courage to walk to the door. As she made her way to the front door, her legs felt weak. She gripped the letter between her fingers.

Just as she was about to knock, Mrs. Hildebrand opened the door. "I've been expecting you," she said.

Looking perplexed Annie stepped back. "You have?" she asked.

Mrs. Hildebrand smiled and reached for Annie's hand. "Oh yes.... you love him," she whispered.

Annie followed her into the kitchen and watched as Mrs. Hildebrand poured two glasses of peach tea. "He's not here right now," she said, placing the glass on the table.

Annie took a sip. "Do you know where he went?"

Mrs. Hildebrand shook her head. "No, he didn't tell me."

Annie frowned. "I really made a mess of things," she confessed.

Mrs. Hildebrand patted Annie's hand. "Nothing that can't be fixed, dear," she said, with a smile.

Annie sighed. "I'm not so sure about that."

The elderly woman cupped her hands around Annie's. "You love him, don't you?"

Annie nodded.

"Then tell him. He needs to hear it."

"I know." Annie fanned the letter. "It's all in here," she explained.

Mrs. Hildebrand raised her eyebrows. "Is that how you think you should tell him?" she asked.

Annie shrugged her shoulders.

Mrs. Hildebrand shook her head. "You need to tell him with your own lips. Speak from your heart." She hesitated before speaking. "Sweetheart, Dan loves you very much. I sat right here until two o'clock this morning, consoling him. You know what he told me?"

Annie shook her head. "No," she whispered.

Mrs. Hildebrand cocked her head to one side. "He said that for the first time in his life, he felt like he really mattered. He said that when you look at him, he feels things he had never felt before." She lowered her voice to a whisper. "He said that when he looks into his future, he sees you."

Annie's eyes widened. "Me?" she whispered.

Mrs. Hildebrand offered a sympathetic smile. "If you love him, don't be afraid to tell him." With those words, Annie clung to the hope he would give her a second chance. She buried her hands in her hair. "What if I tell him and something happens later on? Annie asked.

Mrs. Hildebrand frowned. "You can't live your life afraid to love because of what could happen. I've seen the way you look at each other. I may be old, but I'm not blind. I know love when I see it," she said.

"What if the words come out all wrong?" Annie asked.

Mrs. Hildebrand tapped her chest. "Speak from your heart. He's in love with you and you're in love with him. That's all that matters."

Annie leaned over to hug her. "Thank you," she said, as she stood.

Mrs. Hildebrand pinched Annie's cheek. "Don't you want to wait for him?" she asked.

Annie sighed. "No, I think I know where he may be."

Mrs. Hildebrand watched as Annie backed out of the driveway. She looked up toward the sky and smiled. "They remind me of us when we were young."

****

As Annie drove through the entrance of the park, she searched for Dan's car. "Please let him be here," she whispered. The parking lot was surprisingly full for a weekday. A glimpse of two men walking toward the pavilions caught her attention. From a distance, one of the men resembled Dan.

In an effort to block the brightness of the sun, she shielded her forehead with her hand. Is that him? she wondered. It had to be. He was wearing the same light blue shirt he had on during class.

She was suddenly startled by a flock of geese waddling in front of her car. It was a mother and four little babies. The car jerked when she slammed on her brakes. Luckily, she stopped just in time. As she caught her breath, she watched as they made their way to the grass. The large goose looked at her, as if telling her to watch what she was doing. "Sorry," she whispered.

She parked the car in a nearby space and watched from a distance as Dan and the other man talked. The man was standing across from Dan, with his hands on his hips. Dan's back was toward the parking lot and Annie could see that he had his arms crossed. Who was that with him? She rolled down her window, but the pavilions were too far to hear anything.

Annie squinted as she tried to focus on the other man. He was tall with a medium build and dark hair. She was too far away to see his face. He was dressed in light-colored pants and a yellow golf shirt. He raised his hand to his forehead then placed it back on his hip. Dan just stood there, shaking his head. Annie leaned closer to the windshield. It was apparent they were having a confrontation, but whom would he be arguing with?

She watched in anticipation as the man stepped closer and placed his arms on Dan's shoulders. Dan stepped back, pushing the man's arms away from him. Annie bit the corner of her lip. Should she get out of the car? Just as she was debating about what to do, the man stepped forward and wrapped one arm around Dan's shoulder.

Dan struggled to push the man away, but he didn't move. A moment later, they hugged and the man patted Dan on the back.

"His father," Annie whispered.

They stood in the middle of the pavilion, clinging to each other. Annie smiled as she put the keys in the ignition. As she backed out, she felt guilty for intruding on their private moment, but she felt blessed to have witnessed something that Dan said would never happen.

****

Later that evening, Annie was lying on her bed, staring at the letter she had poured her heart and soul into. She was glad to have the house to herself. The guys at the hardware store convinced her father to fill in for someone on their bowling league. He didn't object as much this time, so she was glad he was starting to enjoy life again. Everyone told her not to push him because he needed time. Although Annie wasn't convinced, her Aunt Susan assured her that he would wake up one day and decide there was more to life and that he had grieved long enough.

Annie stared at the phone. She desperately wanted to call Dan, but it was obvious he had no interest in reconciling. She would wallow in self-pity alone. She missed Kim and the girl talks they used to share. She even missed the little things like their nail appointments. Her entire life had changed since the assignment.

Annie wished she could rewind the clock and go back eight weeks. She wanted to revert to a time when she didn't know about love and broken hearts. Kim was wrong. She wasn't missing anything before by not having a boyfriend. Who needed a broken heart? Who needed love?

She closed her eyes and tried to gather her thoughts. *Oh, who am I kidding? I need love.....I need him.* She felt hopeless.

Annie strolled into the kitchen to get a glass of iced tea. She grabbed a coaster and made her way back to her bedroom.

She was halfway up the steps when she heard a knock at the door. When she walked toward the door, she could see Dan's silhouette through the frosted glass. She took a deep breath and reached for the knob.

As she slowly opened the door, their eyes locked on each other. For a moment, neither of them spoke a word. It was obvious that they were both afraid to make the first move. After a minute of awkward silence, Annie slowly curled her lips into a slight smile.

Dan's eyes traced every detail of her face. She looked more beautiful than ever. He wanted to take her in his arms and tell her how much he missed her. He wanted to tell her that the last week was torture, but he kept his distance. After all, she knew how he felt. He couldn't open himself up to rejection again.

Annie's heart was racing. This is what she wanted.... another chance to see him and tell him how she felt. She continued to hold his gaze. Trembling, she stepped closer to him and hesitated for a moment before wrapping her arms around his neck. Tears flowed from her eyes.

He let out a deep breath, as he pulled her closer. They stood there for several minutes, reveling in the closeness they felt. "Are you okay?" he whispered, as he loosened his grip.

Without letting go, she simply nodded and held him, as he rested his cheek on her head. He pulled her closer.

"I....love you," she whispered.

Closing his eyes, he smiled as feelings of exhilaration surrounded him. He wanted to look into her eyes, but knew that she probably needed a minute. He loved her for admitting it. He knew that saying those words frightened her.

As he stepped back, their eyes locked for a moment, before she looked away.

"Thank you for telling me," he whispered.

She flashed a shy smile. "I didn't think you would come back."

He nodded toward the swing and guided her across the porch. Rather than sitting beside her, he pulled a chair in front of the swing and reached for her hands. He raised his eyebrows, as he studied the expression on her face. He then rubbed her hands, allowing her a moment to gather her thoughts. "Talk to me," he whispered.

She nodded, as she cleared her throat. "I'm so sorry for hurting you. I was afraid to get close to you, but....."

"But what?" he whispered.

She glanced up for a moment but hesitated.

"But what, Annie?"

"I was more afraid of losing you," she said.

He squeezed her hand, as he leaned closer to her face. "Me too," he whispered. "I thought I lost you."

Annie felt a lump in her throat. "I missed you so much," she said.

He tilted her chin, forcing her to look into his eyes. "I didn't want to stay away, you know? Being away from you was torture, but I felt foolish. Annie, I told you that I was falling in love with you, and you didn't' say anything. I felt foolish in thinking that I misjudged our relationship."

She nodded slowly. "I know. I wanted to say it so many times. The truth is…. I think I loved you the minute I first saw you."

Tilting his head, he continued holding her gaze. He was shocked to hear her say that, but immensely flattered. "You want to hear a confession?" he asked.

Annie nodded.

"Remember when I approached you in the courtyard and asked to copy your questions?"

"I remember," she answered.

"Well, remember how I told you someone had torn the pages from my book?"

She raised her eyebrows. "Yes."

He smiled. "I kind of made that up so that I could talk to you," he confessed.

Despite feeling embarrassed, she laughed.

"It's true, and from that moment on I couldn't stop thinking about you."

She held his gaze. "You didn't have to make that up, you know? I would have talked to you."

He laughed until his smile faded into a serious expression. "You're beautiful," he said.

She held her head down and smiled. "Thank you."

"No, thank you," he said.

Annie glanced up. "For what?"

His eyes traced every detail of her face. "For being brave and making me the happiest guy on earth." He pulled her hands close to his chest, forcing her forehead to meet his. "For telling me that you love me," he said.

Annie felt the blood rush to her cheeks. "I meant it. I wrote you a letter, but I didn't have a chance to give it to you."

He smiled. "You did?"

Annie wrinkled her nose. "Yes, but......"

"It's not too late," he said.

"I don't know. It's kind of a moot point now," she said.

"Please, I would really like to read it," he said.

A few minutes later, she returned with the letter. She felt awkward about giving him a note after she had just disclosed her feelings.

He glanced at his watch and smiled. "I better go," he whispered.

They played tug of war with the letter until she finally let go. He pulled her close and gently kissed her lips. "I love you," he whispered.

She held his gaze. "I love you, too."

As he walked to his car, he turned around. "Oh by the way, I'll be going home tomorrow. My Dad and I talked, and they want me to come home."

Annie held her hand to her chest. She didn't want him to know that she had seen him earlier. "I'm happy for you," she said.

He shrugged. "We'll see. I guess it's a start," he said.

Annie smiled, as she rested her head against the door. Her prayers had been answered. She went inside and turned off the porch lights before making her way to her room. As she removed her make-up, she stared at her reflection in the mirror. For the first time ever, she could see her mother's resemblance staring back at her. She smiled. "Everything's okay now Mamma. He came back."

Annie sat on the edge of her bed, debating about whether she should call Kim, but she couldn't wait any longer. Who cared if Darren was with her? This was single handedly the most important thing that ever happened to her and she had to share it with her best friend.

She dialed Kim's number, but barely allowed her to answer before she belted out, "I did it! I told him that I loved him."

"No way!" Kim shrieked.

"I did. Can you believe it?" Annie asked.

Kim laughed. "Well, tell me. I want to hear every detail."

Annie sighed. "Oh, Kim, there is so much to tell. I almost lost him."

"Go on…" Kim said.

Annie told her about the letter and her conversation with Mrs. Hildebrand. "I think he's the one," Annie confessed.

"The ONE?" Kim shrieked.

"Yeah, I think so. You know me better than anyone else and you know I have never felt this way about anyone, but he's….special," she admitted.

Kim was silent for a moment. "Annie, I'm so happy for you. Dan seems like he's the real deal."

"He is," Annie agreed.

Kim giggled. "Well, maybe we can have a double wedding."

Annie laughed. "I take it that things are going well for you and Darren."

"Yeah, Darren's a great guy. He's been so patient and caring with Jill. It's really amazing how much she's changed."

Annie witnessed this first hand. Jill had really turned her life around. She had become involved with the youth group at church and her social circle was much more appealing than before. "You know it's really ironic," Annie said.

"What?" Kim asked.

"You and Darren needed Jill to complete the assignment, right?"

"Yeah, and..?" Kim asked.

"Well, as it turned out Jill needed you just as much," Annie explained.

Kim twirled the phone cord around her finger. "I never thought about it that way."

Annie was silent for a moment. "Think about it. It wasn't coincidental. I think it was all part of God's plan. He knew that you and Darren could help her just like Dan and I helped Mrs. Hildebrand. "I know she's old, but she's been like a mother to me. I can't help but wonder if she was placed in my life for a reason."

Kim detected a contentment in Annie's voice; something she had longed for her friend.

She was ecstatic that Annie had become close to Mrs. Hildebrand. "Maybe you're right," Kim said.

"I have to believe it," Annie said.

Kim continued listening while Annie joyfully reiterated her special moment with Dan.

Annie confided in Kim about her feelings for Dan and how she hoped his relationship with his parents would improve. Annie prayed that his parents would show him the love he deserved and needed.

****

After Dan returned to Mrs. Hildebrand's house, they sat at the table, talking for hours about his conversation with his father. He said he felt guilty for leaving, but Mrs. Hildebrand assured him that his place was with his family. He wanted to spend one last night at her house.

She cut two pieces of chocolate cake, as he told her about his father hugging him for the first time in five years. He wanted so badly for things to change for his family and he hoped this was the beginning of something good. Robert's death tore them apart and it was time they stopped dwelling on his death and focused on living again.

Dan confessed to Mrs. Hildebrand that he wanted to go to baseball games with his father and have family meals again. He told her about how his father used to take him and Robert to all of the home games in Florida.

Mrs. Hildebrand smiled at his innocence. She thought he resembled a child at Christmas as he dreamed of a family life again. She knew he desired his father's approval and hoped he would be made to feel like the special person he was. Her heart filled with pride as she watched him savor the last bite of cake.

Dan placed his plate in the dishwasher and hugged Mrs. Hildebrand. He told her he was thankful for her support and understanding. It was because of her that he found the courage to initiate a meeting with his father. Mrs. Hildebrand had a way of persuading him to do things, while allowing him to take credit for the idea.

"Thank you for letting me stay here and for being such a good listener. I'll never forget what you did for me," he said.

She patted his cheek. "The pleasure was all mine. It's been nice having a man in the house again," she said.

He leaned over to hug her. As he said goodnight, he turned around. "Oh, I almost forgot to tell you something."

She raised her eyebrows.

He beamed with pride. "She told me she loved me today."

Mrs. Hildebrand folded her hands together and winked. She never admitted to him about her conversation with Annie, but she knew in her heart things would be fine.

Dan shut the bedroom door and removed the letter from his pocket. He propped two pillows against the headboard and turned on the lamp as he unfolded the letter.

Dear Dan,

It's so hard to believe that eight weeks have passed by so quickly. I have to tell you that the time we spent together has been amazing. Sometimes it feels like it was all a dream. Every day when I wake up, I thank God for placing you in my life. I have been so unfair. I realize that now.

When you told me that you loved me, I was scared. Don't get me wrong, I was ecstatic to hear those words and I felt the same way, maybe even before you did. I was afraid that if I loved you that I would lose you.

When my Mom died, I felt like I couldn't go on. It has taken me a long time to put my life back together and I didn't want to take a chance on losing you. I was afraid that you would move away or find someone else. To be honest with you, I always thought you were out of my league and

too good for me. Yes, it's a poor excuse for pushing you away, but it's the truth.

I have come to the realization (with some help) that being afraid to love someone would guarantee a life of loneliness and misery. I'm so sorry that I hurt you. I have admitted to myself and I'm ready to admit it to you that I am deeply in love with you. You are the first thing that I think of when I wake up and the last thing I think about when I close my eyes. If you can find it in your heart to forgive me, I would like to give you my heart.... all of it.

Love,
Annie

Dan smiled as he held the letter close to his heart. He read it again before he glanced at the clock. It was late, but he had to talk to her. He had to tell her what it meant that she had told him those things. Although hearing her speak the words was wonderful, there was something sweet and genuine about the letter. As he dialed her number, his eyes focused on the last sentence.

"Hello," she answered.

"I'll take it," he said.

She laughed. "Okay...you'll take what?"

"Your heart. I want all of it. Always and forever," he said.

Annie was silent for a moment. "You read the letter."

He cleared his throat. "Yes, and I understand, but I want to make one thing clear to you," he paused, "Don't ever think you're not good enough for me. Annie, you're the best thing that has ever happened to me. Do you understand that?" he asked.

"Uh huh," she responded.

They continued talking for an hour until their minds surrendered to a state of exhaustion, but neither of them wanted to say goodnight. Dan could hear her breathing intensify through the receiver. He was sure that she had fallen asleep. "Annie," he whispered.

"Hmm," she responded in a raspy voice.

"Baby, we need to hang up now and go to sleep," he said.

"Okay," she whispered, in a slumberous voice.

After they hung up, he folded the letter and tucked it neatly in his notebook. This was something he would keep forever.

Mrs. Hildebrand prepared a gourmet breakfast for Dan since this would be his last morning in her house. Tears filled his eyes as he placed his duffel bag at the bottom of the steps. He wiped a tear as he watched her straighten his place mat. It took him a minute to regain his composure before walking into the kitchen. It was obvious she had gone to a great deal of trouble. He inhaled and let out a deep breath. "I knew my nose didn't deceive me," he joked.

She turned around. Although she displayed a smile for his benefit, her eyes couldn't hide the pain. They had become close and he knew she was lonely. Her course actions during their first meetings were barriers to her soul. She was too dignified to let anyone know how much she longed for friendship. He and Annie studied this behavior in psychology and knew she acted this way because of fear. Gertie told them that after George died, Mrs. Hildebrand became reclusive.

Both were silent as they enjoyed stacks of French toast topped with fresh strawberries. When they finished, she followed him to the door. As they stood on her porch, Mrs. Hildebrand knew he was having difficulty leaving. In an effort to lighten the mood, she reverted to her usual bossy tone. "Now, I hope you don't think you're off the hook just because your project is done. There are still plenty of things that need to be done around here."

With tears forming in the corner of his eyes, he forced a smile. "You weren't about to let us forget," he said.

"No, sir! A promise is a promise. I fully expect you and Annie to come back sometime next week. With summer approaching, you two should have plenty of time to get things done," she said with a wink.

"Yes, ma'am. At your service," he laughed.

When he backed out of her driveway, he felt a rush of mixed emotions. How could he feel like he was on top of the world, but at the same time feel like he was dying inside? Shouldn't he be happy? He had a second chance with Annie and his parents wanted him to come home. Although he knew his friendship with Mrs. Hildebrand would continue, he felt like he was turning his back on her.

As he drove through town, he tried to convince himself that she wouldn't want him to feel this way. He felt very emotional because she had taken him in without any hesitation. She stayed up with him, talking, consoling and praying with him when he felt like he couldn't go on. She too would miss those special times.

Annie knew she would only see Dan for a brief moment between classes then he would be going home. She didn't expect to talk to him that night. After all, this would be his first night back home. She decided that she would spend the evening with Mrs. Hildebrand. Her father would be working late and Kim had promised to go to the movies with Jill.

As she walked toward the parking lot, she heard someone yelling. "Annie, wait up."

She turned around to find Dan sprinting across the lawn. He was out of breath, but he managed to kiss her on the cheek. As they walked to their cars, he ran his hand through his hair. She noticed he only did this when he was nervous.

The campus was completely chaotic as students rushed to their cars. Friday afternoon had arrived and everyone seemed anxious to begin the weekend. Annie opened her car door and tossed her books into the passenger seat. As she buckled her seat belt, Dan leaned inside the window. "I'll miss you tonight," he said.

Annie rubbed his arm. "Yeah, me too, but you need to go home."

"I know, but I'll still miss you."

Annie loved the way he was so sincere. "You'll be okay," she said, as she turned the ignition.

"I'll call you tomorrow," he said.

She gave his arm one last squeeze. "Take your time and get things worked out with your parents. If you don't have a chance to call, I'll understand."

He grinned. "That's why I love you so much."

She nodded. "I love you too."

As she drove away, she watched him from her rear view mirror. He stood there waving until he could no longer see her car.

CHAPTER TWENTY

"Let's go shopping," Kim shouted into the receiver. Annie rubbed her eyes. "What time is it?"

"Time for you to get up. Come on, it will be fun. We can get a pedicure then go shopping. I really need to buy a birthday present for Jill," Kim said.

Annie groaned. "Okay, okay. Give me an hour."

"Great. I'll pick you up at 11:00 a.m.," Kim said.

Annie was glad Kim invited her to go to the mall. She missed spending time with her best friend, besides; it would help take her mind off Dan. Although she had seen him the day before, it felt like it had been weeks.

Kim was late as usual. She was nothing like Dan. When Dan said he would be there at nine, she knew that he would be there right at nine. Annie shook her head as she waited by the door. It was too hot to wait outside and Annie rationalized that it could be another half an hour before Kim arrived.

Annie listened to the messages on the answering machine. She knew that Dan wouldn't have left a message, but she was hopeful. She tilted her head from side to side as she listened to her Aunt Susan go on and on about the upcoming family reunion. The next message was from one of her Dad's friends about another bowling night. As she listened to the latter part of the message, she heard Kim blow the horn.

Annie grabbed her purse and locked the door behind her. As she buckled her seatbelt, she turned toward Kim. "I'm so glad we're doing this. I miss him already."

Kim laughed as she glanced at Annie. "Sounds to me like someone is love sick."

Annie squinted her eyes. "Yeah, well, just remember I'm not used to this."

"Don't get so defensive. It's a good thing," Kim said.

Annie smiled. "I'm sorry. It's just hard being away from him."

Kim winked. "Absence makes the heart grow fonder," she said.

They talked non-stop on the way to the mall. Kim parked outside the main entrance since the nail salon was located inside the door. They sat side by side in the oversized chairs as they soaked their feet in the large basins.

"This feels great," Annie said.

"Mmhmm," Kim agreed. "It's hard to believe we haven't done this in eight weeks."

Annie smiled. "Yeah, it feels like old times again."

Kim shook her head. "Hey, what do you think about a cross necklace?"

With her head resting on the back of the chair, Annie turned to focus on her friend. "You mean for Jill?"

"Yeah, I think she would really like it," Kim said.

"I think that's a great idea," Annie said.

After they paid for their pedicures, they walked the entire mall, looking in all of the jewelry stores. The last store, "The Heavenly Dove," had a large display case of crosses. Annie and Kim watched as the owner removed five different pendants from a tray.

They were all so beautiful, but Kim had decided on a fourteen-carat gold necklace with a small gemstone inserted in the middle. "I think she'll really like this one. "Is it possible to have something engraved on the back?" Kim asked.

The sales clerk said it would have to be a small inscription, but it was possible.

"Faith," Kim said. That's all she wanted engraved on the back of the cross. A simple word that meant so much.

The owner smiled and told them it would be ready in an hour. Kim signed the credit card receipt and promised to return in an hour.

They decided to eat lunch while they waited. As they shared an appetizer, Annie described every detail of her conversation with Dan. It had more of an effect than when she explained it to Kim on the phone.

"So, he's back home now?" Kim asked.

Annie nodded. "Yes and it's killing me not to talk to him."

They spent the next hour engaged in deep conversation about the times Annie and Dan spent at the lake. Kim bragged about Jill's progress and how she felt like the teen was a little sister.

"I have really missed this," Annie admitted.

With her elbows on the table, Kim rested her face in her hands. "Do you ever think about what will happen to us after college?" Kim asked.

Annie wrinkled her forehead. "What do you mean?"

Kim shrugged. "I just wondered if you ever gave it any thought. Just promise me that no matter where our lives take us, we will always stay in touch."

Annie shot her a withering look. She had never considered it before. After all, they had always known each other. Wouldn't they still live in their quaint little town? "We'll always be here for each other," Annie said.

Kim shrugged. "Yeah, you're right."

Just as Annie was about to speak, her cell phone rang. She rummaged through her purse to find the phone. As she flipped it open, she smiled. "It's Dan," she shrieked.

Kim raised her eyebrows. "Answer it," she said, motioning to Annie.

Annie pressed the phone against her ear. "Hey... How are you?" There was a long pause. "Tonight?" Annie asked.

Kim looked perplexed. "What's tonight?"

Annie held up her hand. "Okay. Are you sure they don't mind?" she asked. There was another long pause. "Sounds great. I'll see you then."

"Well?" Kim asked.

"That was Dan," Annie said.

Kim rolled her eyes. "Yeah, I got that, but what did he want?" she asked sarcastically.

Annie frowned. "His parents told him to invite me to their house for dinner tonight."

Kim crossed her arms. "And why don't you look happy?"

Annie bit the corner of her lip. "I don't know. I guess I'm kind of nervous. You know.... because of where he lives."

Kim smirked. "You have the chance to go to Gold Ridge Manor. Do you know how many people would love to drive through those gates?"

Annie tucked a strand of hair behind her ear. "I know, I know. It's just...never mind."

"What? Tell me?" Kim pleaded.

Annie hesitated. "I just don't feel comfortable around people like that."

Kim wrinkled her nose. "People like what?"

Annie shrugged. "You know. They're well off. What if they don't think I'm good enough?"

Kim's mouth dropped open. "Not good enough? Annie, why would you say that?"

Annie cocked her head to one side. "You would feel the same way," she whined.

Kim shook her head. "Oh, no, I wouldn't. Besides, you and Dan love each other. Didn't it occur to you that you would have to eventually meet his parents?"

Annie sighed. "Okay, maybe I'm overreacting a little."

Kim smiled. "Look, they are people too. They put their pants on the same way that you do," she said.

Annie nodded. She admired the way Kim never let anyone intimidate her. She longed to have that type of confidence.

During the drive home, Annie barely heard a word that Kim had spoken. She was preoccupied with what she would wear and how she would greet them. Her mind raced with a million thoughts. What if they didn't like her? What if they told Dan not to see her again?

As they pulled into the driveway, Annie reached for the bags from the back seat. "I'm glad we did this. I've really missed our time together," Annie confessed.

Kim smiled. "Me too. It was a fun day."

"See you in the morning?" Annie asked.

Kim nodded. "Yes and remember what I said about his parents. Go over there and have fun. Be confident."

Annie bit the corner of her lip and shrugged. "I'll try."

Kim winked. "Call me when you get home and tell me all about it," she said.

"Believe me, I will," Annie said.

****

Annie searched her closet, but nothing appealed to her. She fanned every piece of clothing as her eyes scanned from left to right. She shifted her weight to one side as she stood with her hand on her hip. Capris, jeans, a skirt? Why was she making this so difficult? It was just dinner.

In complete frustration, she fell backwards on her bed. She stared at the ceiling, imagined everything in her closet, and started the process of elimination again. As she slowly strolled back to the closet, she noticed a small piece of pink fabric sandwiched between two pairs of jeans. It was a pink sundress that she had bought a few months ago. She held the dress against her body and studied her appearance from every angle. It was perfect. Not too dressy, but slightly nicer than Capris and she had the perfect pair of sandals to match.

As she lightly misted herself with perfume, she glanced in the mirror one more time. She felt good. How could they not like her? Her entire appearance signified a young, respectable woman. She took pride in looking like a woman. Surely, they would appreciate the way she looked.

All of her feelings of confidence went out the window when she heard Dan's car approaching. Her stomach began to hurt. She let out a deep breath as she grabbed her purse and made her way down the steps. He was about to knock when she opened the door.

"Wow!" he responded.

Annie raised her eyebrows. "Is that a good wow or a you're too dressed up wow?" she asked.

He laughed softly as he looked her up and down. "It's a you look beautiful wow."

She smiled as she felt a sense of relief. "You're sure it's not too much?"

"I'm sure," he said convincingly.

As they drove through town, Annie twisted her purse strap around her hand so firmly that it made an indentation in her palm.

Dan sensed that she was nervous and tried to lighten the mood. "Did you have fun at the mall?" he asked.

Annie flashed a quick smile. "Yeah, we had a great time."

His eyes narrowed before glancing back toward the road. "You don't have to be nervous," he said.

Annie's eyes widened. "Is it that obvious?

He patted her hand. "It's okay. They're excited to meet you," he said.

"Really?" she asked.

"Yes, really," he insisted.

As they approached the entrance to Gold Ridge Manor, Annie felt a wave of tension sweep through her body. Were they really excited to meet her? Did he tell them that she didn't come from an upper-class family? She watched in anticipation as the guard motioned Dan through the massive iron gates. The road leading into the subdivision was steep. The enormous houses were adorned with beautifully landscaped yards and circular driveways that allowed dual entrances.

As they continued winding through the streets, she imagined that her house was the size of some of the garages and pool houses. It was almost too much to absorb. She started having second thoughts about meeting his parents. Would he believe her if she told him that she suddenly felt ill?

As they approached a cul-de-sac, Dan glanced her way. "We're here," he announced. *Great!* Annie thought. He had the biggest house in the subdivision. No, on second thought, this was no house. It was a mansion. The brick driveway contoured the manicured lawn and a large concrete fountain with a carving of an angel was the focal point. A massive chandelier hung from the center of the porch.

He pulled into the driveway and parked the car. "Shall we?" he asked, as he opened her door.

As they walked hand- in-hand toward the steps, he felt her resistance. *Goodness, what have I gotten myself into?* She thought. Insurmountable fear kept her from taking another step. Her palms were clammy and she felt like she couldn't take another step.

"What's wrong?" he asked. He could see the terror in her eyes.

"I feel so out of place," she retorted. *Oh, no, I didn't really say that did I?* The color washed from her cheeks.

He looked at her with astonishment. "Annie, no…why?"

She shrugged. "I just feel…….."

As he was about to offer words of comfort, the front door opened.

"Ahh, this must be Annie," his father said. She smiled and extended her hand. She was now face-to-face with the man she caught a glimpse of when she went to the park.

"Please come in," he said.

Annie was amazed at the resemblance between Dan and his father. He was a little taller than Dan, but had the same blue eyes and dark hair. He was handsome just like Dan. As they walked through the foyer, Annie was in awe at the enormous spiral staircase. The shine of the black and white marble floor gave the illusion of a wet surface. In the center of the foyer was a round mahogany table with a colossal floral arrangement. The mansion had several large oriental rugs throughout the halls and rooms.

Dan and Annie followed Mr. Wilson into the living room. "Can we offer you something to drink?" he asked.

"Oh no thank you, sir," Annie responded shyly.

When Mr. Wilson smiled, he looked like Dan. His eyes crinkled in the corners the same way that Dan's did. "You were right," he said, patting Dan on the back. They smiled. "Dan said that you were the epitome of a lovely southern belle," his father remarked.

Annie blushed. She knew it was a compliment, but she felt embarrassed nonetheless.

Mr. Wilson smiled. "It's a good trait to have. If you'll excuse me, I'm going to find the Mrs.," he said.

Annie was starting to feel more at ease, but she wondered how his mother would accept her. Dan reached for her hand. "Have a seat," he said, motioning toward the couch.

Annie looked around the room as she sat with her hands neatly placed in her lap.

"See, I told you there was nothing to be nervous about," Dan said.

Annie smiled. Just as she was about to say something, a black streak ran through the living room. "What was that?" she laughed.

Dan shook his head. "That's Bootsie showing off. He does this whenever we have company." Bootsie was a Scottish terrier that Dan's father had brought home eight years ago. "He's a little neurotic," Dan added with a laugh.

Just then, Bootsie came running through the living room again, but this time he jumped in the middle of Annie's lap.

"Bootsie!" a female voice yelled.

Annie looked up. Dan's mother was standing with her hands on her hips. She was a striking woman. As she stood beside her husband, Annie could see that she was almost as tall as he was. She was very thin and her dark hair was cut in long layers that framed her face. She had big brown eyes and a beautiful smile.

"I'm so sorry," she said, snapping her fingers at the dog.

It was apparent to Annie where Dan got his good looks. Both of his parents were beautiful people.

Annie giggled and held up her hands. "It's okay. I love dogs."

Mrs. Wilson made her way toward the couch and extended her hand. "We're very glad to have you," she said.

Annie stood and shook her hand. "Thank you for the invitation. I'm so glad to finally meet you." She was relieved his parents were nice and didn't come across as pretentious. Once again, she felt guilty for being judgmental.

As they talked in the living room, Dan's mother sat on the arm of the chair, next to her husband. Dan was glad his parents were acting intimate toward each other again. Prior to Robert's death, they were inseparable.

"Dan has told us a lot of nice things about you, Annie," Mr. Wilson said.

Annie looked at Dan and grinned. He winked as he watched her expression.

"Thank you, sir. My father and I think highly of Dan," Annie said.

"You don't have to call me, sir," he said.

Dan's mother nodded. "Yes, I'm Karen and this is Robert."

Dan whispered in Annie's ear. "They hate to be called Mr. and Mrs. They associate that with being old," he joked.

"I heard that," his mother said, giving him a diabolic look.

Bootsie ignored his prior chastisement and jumped into Annie's lap again.

"No, no!" Dan's father yelled.

Annie laughed as she stroked Bootsie's head. "Really, it's okay. We used to have a dog, and I miss this," she said.

Dan's mother cocked her head to the side. "Okay, but if he becomes bothersome, make him get down."

They continued talking for a long time and Annie was now at ease. She was glad they didn't ask questions about her mother. She was even more thankful they didn't question her about her father's occupation and where they lived. Annie was proud of her father's hard work, but she wasn't comfortable enough to disclose her personal life.

Dan glanced at the clock. "Dad, can we start cooking?" he asked.

His parents laughed. "He eats us out of house and home," his father joked.

Dan's face turned red and he laughed.

"I'm not the one who gets up in the middle of the night to eat ice cream," Dan said.

His mother raised her eyebrows. "That explains this," she said, patting her husband's stomach.

Dan's mother gave Annie a tour of the house while Dan and his father cooked the steaks. Large cherry furniture filled the five bedrooms. "I'm going to turn this into a nursery," she said, pointing to the bedroom across from the master. "Did Dan tell you our daughter Jen is pregnant with twins?"

Annie's mouth dropped. "No, he didn't tell me. That's wonderful," she said.

"Well, we just found out this morning. I just wish they lived closer," Mrs. Wilson said with a regretful tone.

Annie offered a sympathetic smile. She remembered that Dan had told her Jen and her husband, Mike still lived in Florida. She imagined this was hard on his parents because of the correlation between Florida and the tragedy. "I'm sure they'll visit a lot," Annie said.

Mrs. Wilson squeezed Annie's shoulder. "I sure hope so," she said.

"Mom!" Dan yelled from the foyer.

"We're up here, son." She shook her head and laughed. "You'll have to excuse his manners."

Annie smiled and followed her down the staircase and into the kitchen. Mr. Wilson was cutting into the middle of a steak. "Annie, come see if this is how you like your steak," he said.

Annie's mouth watered as she watched the juices spill onto the plate. She wasn't accustomed to eating Rib-eyes. Her father usually bought patio steaks or whatever was on sale.

"It looks wonderful, Mr..." She caught herself before she finished the sentence.

Dan laughed as he glanced between Annie and his father. "She almost said it, Dad."

Annie smiled. "Can I help you with anything?"

Dan's mother tucked a strand of hair behind her ear as she peeked into the oven. "No thank you, dear. The potatoes are almost done."

As they sat at the dining room table, Annie noticed the beautiful table setting. The napkins and centerpiece matched the plates and it reminded Annie of something that a prestigious home magazine would display.

Dan read her mind and hoped that she didn't feel awkward. "Don't get too used to this.

Next time we'll probably be eating on paper plates," he joked.

Mrs. Wilson shot him a wry smile. "Please don't hold us accountable for anything that comes out of his mouth," she said.

Annie smiled, as she admired his mother's beauty and elegance. She was sophisticated,

but down to earth. Mrs. Wilson dabbed the corner of her mouth with the napkin and looked up.

"I was telling Annie about Jen's news."

Annie took a sip of tea and smiled at Dan. "Yes, that's very exciting. I like the sound of Uncle Dan," she said.

Dan grinned and slapped his hand on his leg. "Yeah, well just wait until the kid calls them Grandpa and Grandma," he said.

Mr. Wilson laughed and pushed his plate back. His expression became serious and he locked his fingers together. "I'm…,we're excited," he said, exchanging glances with his wife. "This is exactly what our family needs."

Mrs. Wilson nodded, as she took one last bite of steak.

"Annie, I'm sure Dan has shared with you that our family has endured a painful tragedy and we haven't dealt with it very well," Mr. Wilson said.

Dan fidgeted with his napkin and frowned. "Dad, not now," he said glancing toward Annie.

Mr. Wilson held up his hand. "No, let me finish, son."

Dan sighed and twisted his lips as he looked at his mother. She winked and reached across the table to pat his hand.

Mr. Wilson continued. "All I'm saying is that we need something good in our lives. This past year has been sheer heartache." He exchanged a glance with his wife, then focused his attention to Dan. "I'm afraid we haven't been fair to our other two children," he continued.

Dan looked up then glanced away. He was ecstatic that things had improved, but embarrassed to be discussing family issues in front of Annie.

Mr. Wilson looked and Dan and realized that he made him feel uncomfortable. He held up a glass of tea. "Anyway, to new beginnings," he said.

After dinner, Dan led Annie into the back yard. A wooden gazebo was situated between a flower garden and pond.

"This is beautiful," Annie remarked.

Dan sat on a wooden bench inside the gazebo while Annie leaned over the edge, staring into the pond. He couldn't take his eyes off her. She looked beautiful the way her eyes followed the fish as they rippled through the water. "Annie," he said, patting the bench.

She sat down beside him and leaned forward, curling her hands around the edge of the bench. Dan turned toward her, pushing a tendril of hair from her face. "Sorry about my Dad airing our family laundry at the table."

Annie met his gaze. "I thought it was sweet," she replied.

He gently squeezed her hand. "I told them that I was madly in love with you," he said.

Her cheeks flushed. Although they had confessed their love to each other, it was as if she was hearing it for the first time. She looked into his eyes. "What did they say?"

He laughed softly. "They said you must be blind."

Annie nudged his arm. "Seriously, what did they say?" she asked.

His smile faded into a serious expression. "They said that it had to be the real thing for me to admit it. My mom said I have always been more reserved than Jen and Robert." He paused for a moment. "They knew all along I would be the one to fall for my first and only love." With those words, he looked away.

Annie loved his honesty, even though he sometimes made her feel uncomfortable. She found it extremely difficult to believe that with his good looks, he never allowed himself to get serious with anyone else. She felt a sense of pride in knowing she was his first and only love.

As the evening drew to a close, they stood in the gazebo, under the stars. The moonlight reflected off the pond and the sound of the water as it splashed down the rocks created a serene feeling. Dan pulled her close. They stared into each other's eyes and without another word; they swayed back and forth as if they were dancing.

"I always hate this time of night," he said.

She drew back and looked into his blue eyes that sparkled in the moonlight. He kissed her cheek and whispered in her ear. "Some day it will be different."

Annie studied his serious expression. "Do you mean?"

Before she could finish the sentence, he gave her a tender smile and nodded. "Annie, I want to be with you forever. I want to look forward to the day when I don't have to take you home because your home will be with me."

Annie froze as she stared into his eyes. She was consumed with bittersweet emotions. He was everything she had dreamed about, yet she felt overwhelmed. Her mind filled with uncertainty. She loved him and he loved her, but would their love survive until they graduated? They had two more years of college.

He sensed her tension and gave her a quizzical look. "Did I say something wrong?"

Her heart tugged with emotion as she stepped back into his embrace. "No," she whispered, then hesitated. "I just don't want to jinx this. You are the best thing that has ever happened to me and I just want to take it slowly."

He strengthened his embrace and whispered into her hair. "Okay, we'll take it slow."

CHAPTER TWENTY-ONE

❧

December 25th, two and a half years later

On Christmas morning, Annie awoke to a sweet aroma permeating from the kitchen. She knew she should make her way downstairs to wish her father a Merry Christmas, but she wanted to relish another minute under the warm comforter. As she gathered the covers under her chin, she tried to imagine what the big gift was that Dan had talked about for two weeks. She initially thought he had purchased an engagement ring, but he told her that her present was too big to put in a box.

Despite her obnoxious begging and pleading, he never provided a hint. She played a guessing game every night since Thanksgiving, but he just smiled as she tried to coax him into telling her. Annie felt sure she could persuade Kim into disclosing the big secret, but she had no luck. Kim assured her that Dan never mentioned anything to her. Annie believed her because she knew that Kim never kept a secret. She pondered on their last conversation.

"He's tricking you Annie. It's an engagement ring, but he's not going to tell you," Kim said convincingly.

"No, I really don't think so. Dan said he wouldn't have enough money saved until next spring."

Kim sighed. "You're so naïve. Do you really think he needs more time to save money?

He's rich…remember?"

Annie threw back the covers and sat on the edge of her bed. Just as she slipped her feet into her fuzzy slippers, the phone rang. Before she could reach across the nightstand to pick up the receiver, it stopped ringing. She figured her father had answered. Her Aunt Susan called every year to wish them a Merry Christmas.

Just as she put on her robe, her father tapped on the door. "Annie," he whispered, as he opened the door slowly.

"Merry Christmas, Daddy." She couldn't help but laugh at the white powder that covered her father's robe. He didn't cook much, but when he did, it was obvious.

"Merry Christmas to you too sweetheart. Oh, Dan called but I told him that you were still sleeping and he insisted that I not wake you."

Annie smiled and raised her eyebrows. "Are you cooking something?"

He looked down and dusted the powder from his robe. "As a matter of fact, I am. Apple Cinnamon muffins."

Annie looked surprised. "I'm impressed," she said.

He rubbed his chin. "Yeah, well, it wasn't too difficult to add an egg and some water,"

he joked.

Annie's smile faded. "Dad, can I ask you a question?"

"Of course, Honey, what is it?"

Annie hesitated. "Do you think Dan will ever ask me to marry him?" She could feel her face heat up and part of her wished she wouldn't have asked him.

"Oh, Annie," he said, as he leaned his head against the doorway. "I have no doubt that Dan will ask you to marry him."

Before she could say anything, he walked over and sat on the edge of her bed. "Annie, aren't you the one who told him several times that you wanted to take things slowly?"

She looked down. "I know, but it's been six months since we graduated and now that he has his own practice, I just assumed."

Before she could finish, her father patted her hand. "Honey, I'm sure you have nothing to worry about. If I know Dan, he's making sure that you two will be financially stable before he proposes."

Annie bit the corner of her lip. She knew her father was probably right because even though Dan was a romantic at heart, he was very practical.

Annie and her father ate breakfast, as they reminisced about her mother and how things used to be. There were moments that they laughed so hard they could barely catch their breath, but reality soon set in and they sat there in silence, exchanging glances.

The day seemed to pass by quickly and it was almost time to start getting ready to go to Dan's house for Christmas dinner. Dan's parents invited Annie's father and despite his reservations, he agreed to join them. Annie couldn't bear the thought of leaving him at home, alone, on Christmas.

Her heart burst with pride when she saw her father walking down the steps in his black suit. He looked so handsome and it reminded her of the Sunday mornings when her mother was alive and they went to church as a family. She missed those times and wished that her father would start going to church again. He loved getting dressed up.

"You look really nice, Dad," she said straightening his tie.

He gave her a wink and told her to wait in the car while he grabbed the keys. She wondered if he needed a minute to himself.

As they drove to Dan's house, her father spoke very few words. She wondered if he was dreading the evening more than he let on. Annie was grateful to Dan and his parents for extending the invitation to her father because although she tried very hard to mimic the big Christmas dinners that her mother prepared, it just wasn't the same.

Every year, her Aunt Susan, invited them to her house, but her father always declined by making up excuses not to go. She knew this had to do with his guilt of abandoning memories. He had come a long way during the last few months and she was glad he started spending time with old friends, but holidays were hard for him.

When they pulled into Dan's driveway, her father glanced at the mansion that was adorned with strands of white lights. Fancy wreaths hung from every window and red bows and garlands draped from the second-floor balcony. As they walked toward the entrance, he hesitated and tears filled his eyes. His voice trembled. "Your mother would have loved this, Annie."

Annie remembered how her mother always enjoyed driving around to look at the Christmas lights. She especially enjoyed driving through the high-class neighborhoods and fantasizing about what the houses looked like inside. Annie touched her father's hand and told him how much she loved and admired him for his loyalty to her mother's memory. She wiped a tear from the corner of his eye and kissed him on the cheek.

Just as Annie reached for the doorbell, Dan opened the door and smiled. "Mom, do we know these two people," he joked.

"Very funny," Annie responded, as she gave Dan a friendly hug.

"Hello," Mrs. Wilson chimed in behind Dan. "Jack, we are so pleased that you could make it."

Annie's father patted Mrs. Wilson's hand. "I am very grateful for the invitation," he said with complete sincerity.

"Dan, please take their coats," she said, as she led Annie's father into the living room. She looked so beautiful in her green velvet pantsuit.

Mr. Wilson was sitting in a chair talking with Dan's grandfather about a recent investment that he made. The house was filled with Christmas cheer. The aroma of gingerbread permeated the air and the crackle of wood burning in the fireplace created a cozy atmosphere. The foyer displayed two life-sized nutcracker statues on each side of the entrance and mistletoe hung from every doorway. The cherry spiral staircase could have won an award for a real masterpiece. Poinsettias cascaded down each step and the railings were wrapped with garland and white lights. The sound of Christmas music somehow made the large house feel inviting.

Dan and Annie walked hand-in-hand into the living room and stood by the fire. Bootsie donned a red sweater and he was too preoccupied with chewing a stuffed animal to notice they had company. Annie's father snapped his fingers to get Bootsie's attention. It was obvious how much he missed having a dog. When Barney disappeared, it was the second most traumatic moment in his life. Annie was delighted when Dan suggested getting her father a puppy for Christmas. She adored Dan for his kindness and regard for others.

Annie's father laughed, as Bootsie grabbed the toy and lunged into his lap.

Mrs. Wilson placed her hand on her hip. "Bootsie! Get down!"

Annie's father held up his hand to imply that it was okay. It was obvious that he enjoyed having a dog in his lap again.

"He thinks he's human and that everyone loves him," Mrs. Wilson said, apologetically.

She excused herself and returned a few minutes later with a tray of appetizers. Annie thought the display looked as delicious as the food. Mrs. Wilson was accustomed to throwing parties and she had every type of serving platter that one could imagine.

With all of the holiday chaos, nobody noticed that Jen and Mike were standing in the doorway of the foyer. They were holding the twin boys, Brandon and Brendon.

"Hello," Jen announced from a distance.

Mrs. Wilson looked up and ran to the foyer with her arms extended. "There are Grandma's babies." The twins were wearing oversized coats and the hoods camouflaged all but their noses and mouths. They rubbed their sleepy eyes as Mrs. Wilson helped Mike remove their coats.

She took turns kissing each child repeatedly. "Let's go see what Santa Claus brought you," she said, as she led them to the Christmas tree.

Jen and Mike greeted everyone with a hug and Annie was touched that they included her father. Jen was outgoing and had a lot of her mother's characteristics. Mike, on the other hand, was very quiet and reserved. He sat down on the floor and watched the boys touch all of the presents. "Don't tear the paper," he warned them.

Annie's father watched in amazement as the boys chased Bootsie through the living room. "What I would give to have that kind of energy," he said.

Mrs. Wilson and Jen walked into the kitchen to check on the meal. Annie felt guilty for not offering to help, but she didn't want to impose on their time together. She remembered the special times that she spent alone, with her mother. She wanted Jen to have the same memories with her mother. Besides, Mrs. Wilson had been excited for weeks knowing she would get to see them.

A few minutes later, they returned to the living room, carrying platters of food.

"Dinner is ready," Jen announced, in a cheerful tone.

The dining room table was decorated exquisitely. Every seating had several pieces of china with red napkins and freshly polished silver. Mrs. Wilson even placed decorative nametags on each plate. Annie could sense her father's discomfort, as he glanced at all the silver. She still had trouble remembering which fork to use. Her family was very informal and never entertained on this level. Annie was thankful for her mother's simplicity. She was domesticated, but very common.

As they took their seats, Dan's grandfather abruptly interrupted. "Why do we need three forks?" he asked.

Everyone laughed at his uncouth burst of honesty. Mrs. Wilson folded her hands and smiled. "Dad doesn't agree with our style of entertaining."

He elbowed Annie's Dad. "That's the good thing about being old. You can say whatever you think."

Annie's father laughed. "I imagine so," he said.

Dan's mother tucked a strand of hair behind her ear as she flashed her father a wry smile before glancing toward her husband. "Honey, would you like to say the blessing?" she asked.

Mr. Wilson said a beautiful prayer and thanked God for allowing them to be together. "Amen," everyone echoed in unison. Annie was especially pleased that Mr. Wilson thanked God for allowing her father to join them.

Dinner was excellent in every aspect. It was apparent that Mrs. Wilson spent several days planning and cooking the gourmet meal and every dish looked as appetizing as it tasted. The conversation ranged from Christmas to the rising costs of tuition. Dan's grandfather talked about how Christmas had changed from the time he was a child to how commercialized it had become.

After dessert, everyone assembled in the living room as Dan and Mike passed out the gifts. Annie's father looked surprised as Dan handed him a gift from his parents.

"Oh, you shouldn't have," he said, as he slowly removed the bow and placed in on the armrest of the chair.

Everyone else ripped open the packages in a matter of seconds, but Annie's father took his time. He was over-whelmed with the generosity of Dan's family.

"Geez, Jack, don't you have that present opened yet," Mr. Wilson joked.

"I'm working on it," he laughed.

The twins seemed to be more interested in the paper and bows than the actual presents.

Brandon was stomping his feet inside a large box while Brendon placed the lid on top of his head. Bootsie was buried in the wrapping paper and everyone laughed as they watched the ball of paper come to life.

Dan leaned down and whispered in Annie's ear. Her heart began to pound as she waited for him to return with the puppy. He returned a few minutes later with a big green box and a beautiful silver ribbon. The box had four little holes on the backside and she watched in anticipation as Dan walked into the living room. "I found this present in the basement and it has Jack's name on it."

Annie's father looked at Dan with utter amazement, as he pointed his thumb toward his chest.

"Yes, it's from us," Annie confessed.

Dan placed the box on the floor. Annie's father glanced around the room before opening the gift. As he lifted the top of the box, the little Beagle puppy started jumping around.

The twins squealed as they noticed the puppy. "Puppyyyyyyyyy," Brendan said, as he clapped his hands together.

Annie's father laughed as he reached down to retrieve the puppy from the box. "Well, I'll be… "I can't believe you kids did this for me," he said.

Annie's eyes filled with tears as she watched her father hold the puppy. For the first time in a very long time, he looked genuinely happy.

The twins ran over to see the puppy. "Hold, hold," Brandon said.

"Don't hurt him, Mrs. Wilson said. "Pet him softly."

"Sofwey," Brendon muttered, as he stroked the puppy's head.

Annie rested her head on Dan's shoulder. "This is the best Christmas ever," she whispered.

He leaned down and whispered in her ear. "The best is yet to come."

Annie smiled as she studied his expression, but she couldn't determine what he meant.

Although he told her they would have to wait until spring to get engaged, she hoped it was all a farce. She was ready to make it official.

Annie's father stood up as he held the puppy close to his chest. "I can't thank you enough for your hospitality. I really enjoyed myself," he said.

Mrs. Wilson held her hand on her chest. "It was our pleasure," she said.

Mr. Wilson extended his hand. "Yes, we enjoyed it very much. You'll have to come again soon."

Annie's father agreed. "Well, I better get this little guy home," he said, as he kissed Annie on the cheek.

Annie smiled and rubbed the puppy's paw. She thought it was strange that her father didn't ask her what time she would be home, but she assumed he was too consumed with the excitement of his new friend.

Dan gripped Annie's shoulders as he followed her father. "Wait here, Annie. I'm going to walk your father to his car."

Annie watched them from the window. They shook hands then her father patted Dan on the back before getting in the car. Dan's hand was resting on the car door and he turned toward the window then back to her father. Annie wondered what was taking so long and what they were talking about. It seemed like they talked forever.

A few minutes later Dan entered the house. His cheeks were flushed from the cold. He flashed a smile at Annie. "Are you ready to get out of here?" he asked.

Annie shook her head. "Yes. Was Dad okay? You two talked for a while."

He gently kissed her on the cheek. "Yes, he's fine. Just do me a favor and wait here one more minute. I'll be right back."

He returned a few minutes later wearing a black leather jacket and it was obvious he freshened his cologne. He ran his fingers through his hair as they said goodnight to his parents.

They held hands as they walked down the sidewalk. When they approached his car, he opened the door for Annie and knelt down as he helped her with the seat belt. His eyes were shining, as he lifted her hand to his lips. "Are you ready for your present?" he asked.

Annie wanted to tell him that she was more than ready, but she was too anxious to speak.

Dan reached into his pocket and removed a scarf. "You're going to have to wear this around your eyes until we get there," he explained.

Annie wrinkled her forehead and leaned away from him. "Where are we going?" she asked.

"Just trust me on this Annie and cover your eyes."

She held up her hand to stop him from putting the scarf around her eyes.

"Trust me," he whispered in her ear, as he slowly tied the scarf around her head. "Okay, lean back now and relax. We'll be there in a few minutes," he said.

Annie's mind raced with a million thoughts as they drove to the secret destination. Dan didn't say a word, but Annie could sense that he glanced her way several times. Her palms were sweaty and her breathing accelerated. The scarf hid all traces of light. Her sense of smell became more prevalent as she breathed in the clean smell of his cologne. She lost all sense of direction, but she knew they had driven for several miles.

She felt the car slow down and the sound of the turn signal made her heart race even faster. They had reached their destination, but where were they? Dan removed the keys from the ignition and although she couldn't see anything, she knew he was sitting there in silence. After what appeared to be several minutes, he reached over and gently held her hand. "We're here," he said.

Annie felt like her heart would beat right out of her chest while she sat there in silence, not knowing what was happening. "Can I take this off now?" she asked.

He pulled her hand down. "Not yet. Just sit still."

Dan closed his car door and she could hear his footsteps getting closer to the passenger side. He opened her door and unbuckled the seat belt. "I'm going to help you out of the car. Let me guide you," he said.

Annie felt the frigid temperature against her face. Her body tensed as her lungs filled with cold air. Dan slowly walked her around the car and placed himself behind her. Her heart continued to race as his hands untied the scarf. When he removed the scarf, she blinked several times, allowing her eyes to adjust. They were standing in front of a beautiful two-story Cape Cod house with a wraparound porch. The front yard displayed a white picket fence and a brick walkway. A light snow covered the bushes, but the streetlights provided enough radiance to see the beauty of the house.

Annie glanced at the house then looked at Dan with a confused expression.

"It's ours, Annie," he said, guiding her closer to the house.

Her eyes widened, but she was at a loss for words. Shock was more like it. She had never imagined that the big surprise was a house. "Ours?" she asked, as she struggled to speak.

He shook his head and stared into her eyes. "Yes, baby, it's ours," he whispered.

Tears flowed down her cheeks as she began to sob. "It's so beautiful... I, I can't believe this is ours," she said.

Dan wrapped his arms around her and held her for a few minutes until she regained her composure. "Let's go inside where it's warm and you can see the rest of the house."

Annie's mouth dropped as they stepped inside the foyer. The house was amazing.

Hardwood floors extended throughout the entire first floor, and the kitchen was unbelievably exquisite. Granite countertops complimented the massive cherry cabinets. Annie was in awe at the thought of living in the house. She stood in the kitchen, examining the very place they would prepare meals.

"Annie come see the living room," Dan said.

Annie stood in front of the enormous rock fireplace that was surrounded by an elegant mahogany mantel. Dan leaned down to ignite the gas logs. They watched as shadows from the fire danced on the wall. In the corner of the room was a small Christmas tree with two presents neatly tucked under the bottom branches. As they explored the rest of the house, Annie envisioned what their future would hold. She imagined having their first meal together in their new home. She imagined sitting by the fire on a cold day.

As he led her into the master bedroom, she imagined what it would be like to spend their first night in the house as husband and wife. She thought that Dan must have wondered the same thing because he flashed a bashful smile. She felt a wave of embarrassment run through her. The thought of everything that encompassed a marital relationship left her feeling overwhelmed. She felt unnerved standing in the bedroom and Dan sensed her discomfort. She was thankful that he shared her strong morals and beliefs. Not once did he pressure her into anything. He had always remained a gentleman and she knew their wedding night would be special. God had brought them together and their love was strong.

"Annie, wait here for a minute," he said. He returned a few minutes later and guided her back into the living room. He opened the hall closet and removed a quilt. Annie watched as he unfolded the quilt and spread it in front of the fireplace. He extended his hand as she walked closer to him. He pulled her against him with one hand and held her face with the other.

"I thought tonight would never get here," he said.

Annie stared into his eyes. "I never imagined this," she said.

He smiled. "I take it you like it." he said.

"Are you kidding?" she asked. "This is so much more than I ever dreamed of."

He smiled. "What do you like most about the house?"

Annie shook her head. "Oh, gosh. I love everything about it," she said.

Dan was silent for a moment as he glanced from the fire to Annie. "You want to know what I love most about the house?" he asked.

Annie raised her eyebrows and nodded.

"I like the memories that we're going to make, starting tonight," he said.

As they knelt on the rug, Dan reached under the tree and handed a small package to Annie. "This is from Mrs. Hildebrand," he said.

Annie gave him a quizzical look.

"She wanted us to open it tonight," he explained.

Annie removed the tissue paper from the box while Dan craned his neck to see what was inside. "What is it?" he asked.

Her eyes filled with tears as she removed the glass figurine. "It's the missing piece to the carriage."

Before Annie could speak another word, Dan chimed in. "The bride and groom."

Annie gently rubbed the figurines. "This is what she meant when she said that someday she would give me the missing piece." A teardrop spilled onto the carriage as Annie held the figurine close to her chest.

Dan pulled her close as they admired the figurine. As he released his grip, he pointed to the other package under the tree. "I think that will go nicely with it," he said.

Annie stared at the package. She couldn't imagine what was in the large box.

"Go ahead," he said, handing her the gift.

She smiled as she neatly removed the paper. Inside the large box was a smaller velvet box. Annie's heart began to pound as she opened the lid. She gasped as her hand flew to her mouth. Tears flowed down her cheeks. Reluctant to believe her eyes, she glanced between Dan and the box. "It's Mrs. Hildebrand's ring," she cried.

Dan's eyes filled with tears as he removed the ring from the box and knelt in front of her. Annie was laughing and crying hysterically.

"Annie, will you do me the honors and marry me?"

She threw her arms around his neck and cried into his shoulder. "Yes, yes, I will marry you!"

CHAPTER TWENTY-TWO

As she stood looking at her reflection in the mirror, Annie felt anxious and overwhelmed. Today was a special day, one that she had dreamed about ever since she was a little girl. She wanted every detail to be perfect, just like she had rehearsed it in her mind at least a million times.

As her eyes traced down the beautiful white satin gown that her mother had worn almost twenty -five years earlier, she recited the old adage "Something old, something new, something borrowed, something blue." She smiled as she flared the dress and twirled to look at every angle of the beautiful gown. "Something old, but very special," she whispered.

As she straightened her veil, sunlight peeked through the blinds and reflected off her diamond. Tears filled her eyes as she extended her hand to examine the beautiful ring. She now understood the saying that God never closes one door without opening another. Four years ago, she felt like life had cheated her. God had provided her with the strength to walk through the open door.

Annie wiped the tears from the corner of her eyes as she heard a knock on the door. "Come in," she said. She expected the door to open, but it didn't. Annie slowly opened the door and looked down the corridor of the church, but nobody was there. As she stepped back, she looked down and saw a long white box lying on the floor. She looked down the hall again, but there was silence. Kim had gone to get Annie some water and the other bridesmaids were on their way. Annie picked up the box and closed the door.

As she opened the box, she began to sob. There were two dozen yellow roses neatly tucked inside. She removed one and lifted it to her nose. As she took a deep breath, she inhaled the sweet fragrance of the flower. She looked inside the box for a card, but she only found the flowers and baby's breath neatly wrapped in green tissue paper.

The two hours before the ceremony passed by quickly. Kim and the bridesmaids gathered around Annie as the photographer took pictures. Moments later, Annie could hear the sound of the piano and knew her father would be coming to get her. When he caught a glimpse of his little girl, tears flowed down his cheeks. His voice was hoarse as he grasped for words.

"How do I look, Daddy?" she asked.

He rested his forehead on hers. "You look absolutely beautiful. Just like your mother," he whispered.

Annie wiped the tears from the corner of his eye. "I love you so very much. I couldn't have asked for a better father," she said.

As he escorted her down the aisle, she paused to give Mrs. Hildebrand a yellow rose before making her way to the front. The elderly woman was frail and her health was declining, but she was determined to attend the wedding. She loved Annie and Dan with all her heart.

The church was filled with yellow flowers and the bridesmaids wore yellow dresses that Annie was sure her mother would have loved. When the preacher asked, "Who giveth this woman?" Annie kissed her father on the cheek.

Dan and Annie exchanged vows in front of God and all of their friends and families. They vowed to love each other unconditionally for the rest of their lives.

Annie never found out who sent the yellow roses, but she knew in her heart where they came from. As the limo pulled away from the church, Annie whispered something to the driver as she twirled the rose in her hand.

As they made their way through town, the limousine slowed down and turned onto the gravel road beside the cemetery. Annie rubbed the rose across her cheek and smiled. As the driver opened the door, Dan stood beside the car and watched his new bride place a single yellow rose on her mother's grave. She turned around to look at him. He never said a word, but his smile let her know that he understood.